AF429493

BOOK TWO IN THE *DARKNESS* TRILOGY

THE
ABYSS

REBECCA HAMBY

Rebecca Hamby
The Abyss Book Two in The Darkness Trilogy
Copyright @ Rebecca Hamby 2023

All rights reserved. No part of this book may be reproduced or transmitted in any form without written consent from the author, except by a reviewer who may quote brief passages for review purposes only.

This is a work of fiction. Names, characters, places, and incidents are used fictitiously and are a product of the authors own imagination.

Cover Design: Pink Elephant Designs
Interior Formatting: Pink Elephant Designs
Editor: Rosanna Chiofalo Aponte

Dedicated to

The little girl who never in a million years thought they would be writing her second dedication page. Even when you fell into the deep dark abyss of sadness, you persevered and fought like hell to survive. You held on to the tiniest bit of light and didn't let the darkness consume you. You are stronger than you think and will never let the heavy blanket of your demons swallow you. Keep fighting, you are worthy of the light that sometimes disappear.

PLAYLIST

Hold On - Chord Overstreet
Middle of The Night – Loveless
Your Guardian Angel – Red Jumpsuit Apparatus
Wherever You Will Go – The Calling
Love is Gone – Slander, Dylan Matthew
Animal I Have Become – Three Days Grace
Can You Feel My Heart – Bring Me The Horizon
You Made a Monster – Nick Kingsley, Hannah Hart
The Death of Peace of Mind – Bad Omens

CHAPTER 1

SLOAN

I've never been scared of the dark. It's my safe place, the place I can't be seen; therefore, no one can hurt me. Or so I thought. Darkness, to me, is something tangible. I can feel it in my hands, in my core, in my mind. It's a thick, inky black liquid that finds its way into even the smallest of crevices until you're so full it has nowhere else to go. You are no longer in the dark- ness; you've become the darkness.

I've always embraced the darkness, rather than fearing it. However, it wasn't until I could no longer see Dean's lifeless body beneath me, that I tried to fight off the darkness that was quickly pulling me under. Fuck.

My head was pounding and there's a slight ringing in my left ear, annoying the fuck out of me. When I opened my eyes, I couldn't focus on anything. My vision was so blurry I found myself blinking over and over to try and regain my eyesight. I was lying down, pushing myself up to a sitting position. I rubbed my eyes with the palms of my hands. Once I was able to see my surroundings, I found that I was alone. I was alone in what looked to be a hospital room, but not exactly. Everything was white. The walls, the door, the bed that I was sitting on. I swung my legs over the side of the bed. I felt a tug in the crook of my right arm. Looking down I saw an IV was inserted, and I followed the line that was attached to a bag of clear fluids. Reading the bag, I saw that the contents of the bag read "saline."

Where the actual fuck was I? And where was Dean? I looked across the room and saw there was a small table that contained bandages, tape, scissors, and more bags of fluid. Taking a few deep breaths, I looked down at my body and saw that I was now in a pair of sweatpants and a loose white T-shirt. Someone dressed me? As my breathing started to speed up, I felt scraping underneath my shirt. Pulling it up, I saw that where each of the cigar burns I'd been given, was a bandage with a clean, white gauze fastened with tape. I was definitely in the hospital, wasn't I?

I stood from the bed and ripped the IV line from my arm, eager to leave and try to find Dean. The room was fairly small, so it only took me three long strides to get to the door. Grabbing the handle, I twisted the knob and swung the door open. Panic instantly swept over my body as my eyes locked onto a man in all black, with a black ski mask pulled down covering his face. I screamed. Stepping back into the room, I started swinging my arms trying to defend myself.

"Oww! Owww, love! It's me; it's Colson." He pulled his mask off, revealing his gorgeous face. He looked like he hadn't slept in days. He had dark rings under his eyes, and the making of a bruise on his left cheek bone. The purplish color deepened into a black mass of pooled blood underneath his skin. He closed the gap between us and wrapped his arms around me so tight, I had to release the breath in my lungs.

I was breathing so fast I thought I might faint, but the moment Colson's arms encased my body I collapsed into his arms. My eyes were burning with unshed tears, and I could no longer hold them back. I sobbed into his chest as we both fell to the ground. He held me in his lap for a long moment, letting me release all the emotions I had held while at the warehouse. He just sat there with me, whispering reassurances in my ear as I sobbed.

"Where are we? How did you find me? Where is Dean?" I had so many questions. I pushed off his chest, meeting his tired eyes. "Where is Dean? Is he okay?" He didn't answer me right away; he just stared into my eyes and pushed a loose strand of my hair behind my ear. Had he died in the warehouse? It was in that moment, that moment of possibly losing Dean, that I began to realize how much these guys meant to me. More tears flooded my eyes, and Colson wiped one away with his thumb before answering me.

"He'll survive, but he is in pretty bad shape. He lost a lot of blood, but he's in the middle of a transfusion as we speak." His voice was low, not a whisper, but low enough to sound like he was worried himself.

"Where are we? Are we in the hospital?" I asked, looking around the room we were now sitting in the middle of.

He brushed his hair back with his hands and looked around the room. "No, we are at a secret location that is a makeshift hospital for employees of The Shadows." This time he was whispering. "Listen, Sloan, you are not supposed to be here, only people of the organization are allowed in this facility. There was an exception made tonight, due to Dean's involvement. You've been treated by our physician and given fluids for dehydration. Now that you are bandaged up, we need to get you out of here as quickly as possible." He raised himself off the floor, pulling me up beside him and quickly started making his way to the door.

"Wait, I need to see Dean first. I can't leave without seeing him with my own eyes." I pulled my hand from his, then froze. He turned and stared at me, understanding, with worry written clearly across his beautiful face. He sighed heavily as he thought about his answer. He then pulled some black fabric from his back pocket.

"This needs to be quick, Sloan. We are already pushing it with you being here. Come here. I need to put this blindfold on you before leaving this room." He made his way behind me, and when he reached up to place the blindfold, I grabbed his wrists, forcing him to stop.

"You can trust me, baby girl, I'm not going to hurt you." His voice was soothing in my ear, but a feeling of unease passed through me. Why was he blindfolding me?

As if he read my mind, Colson said, "We can't take the chance of you seeing any other Shadow employees, and you are not authorized to see the inside of this facility. We took a risk with you seeing this room, but I couldn't bear you waking up to being blindfolded. So, I waited outside your door until you woke up. Please, let me put this on before someone sees you." He genuinely sounded worried, so I dropped the hold I had on his wrist and allowed him to blindfold me. Shit. Here was the darkness once again.

"Hold my hand. I will direct you to where Dean is, but please don't say a word." Grabbing his hand, I nodded my response. I heard the sound of the door opening as a cool draft of air hit my body. I shivered in response, or maybe from nervousness, but started walking when Colson pulled at my arm gently. We walked slowly as our feet padded against the tile floor. I wasn't wearing any shoes and the tile was like walking on blocks of ice.

We turned left and continued down a long,

straight corridor, and then took a right followed by another right. How big was this fucking place? Another long corridor later, he pulled my arm to the left and stopped abruptly.

"Okay, love. We are right in front of Dean's room, please don't make any loud noises—just whisper. I will take off your blindfold as soon as we are inside. Just know he looks worse than he feels. Dean is a tough motherfucker. Don't let his condition fool you."

With that I heard the sound of a door opening. Colson's hand pressed on my lower back, ushering me inside. Taking two steps inside, I stopped—my heart pounding. The sound of the door latching and a deadbolt turning indicated we were now securely locked inside. Colson slowly untied my blindfold, and when he dropped it away from my face, I had to blink several times to regain my focus. When I finally could see properly, I was not emotionally ready for what I saw.

"Dean…" I cried.

CHAPTER 2

SLOAN

Dean lay unconscious on an identical bed as I woke up. Tucked in under white sheets, IV draped over the bed spread with reddish-brown fluid entering his veins. I followed the tubing and saw he was receiving AB+ blood. He was utterly still, except for the slight rise and fall of his chest, allowing me some sort of relief that he was indeed alive. He looked as if he was teetering on the edge of death. His once sun-kissed golden skin was now an ashen pale, from what I assumed was the blood loss.

He was covered in bandages, hiding the evidence of the many cigar burns that would forever pepper his beautiful torso. The greenish-purple bruises littered his skin from his eyes to his chest. I couldn't see much further below his waist since his blanket was covering him. I walked over to his bedside, feeling the sting of tears filling my eyes. Standing beside him, I looked down at his battered face and couldn't help the many tears that slid down my cheeks.

I grabbed his hand gently and interlaced our fingers together. Lowering my head, I couldn't help the sob that escaped my throat. Covering my mouth with my other hand to try and contain my cries, a strong but gentle hand rested on my shoulder. I didn't even have to turn to look to see if it was Everett. His touch makes me feel secure and grounded. His touch is rough like Dean's, but also tender and soothing like Colson's. He's the perfect combination of a dominating alpha and a freshly stuffed teddy bear.

It's amazing to me that I've only been with these guys for five months and I can already identify them simply by their touch. They've each etched a piece of their souls into my heart that will forever be a part of me. Five months is all it took for me to fall for all three of them. They are mine and I'm theirs. A family of sorts that is far from traditional, but it has become our norm.

I can't imagine sharing my heart with three separate men, but what Everett, Dean and Colson have created is a sense of safety, something I've never felt in my short existence. They care for me which they've shown by saving my life more than once. We've all become this unit, this team, and for me, at least, I feel like these guys are now my family. I hope they feel the same.

"He was shot twice? Once on the bike and again in

the warehouse." My voice was low, so as to not wake Dean.

"He was shot with a rubber bullet on the bike." Everett's tone was laced with exhaustion, as if he'd been awake for days. His voice was gravelly, hoarse, and dry. "They wanted to keep him alive but unconscious, making it easier to transport the two of you. They wanted him alive when he was tortured, and to witness you being tormented as well," Colson said near the door as he watched his brother motionless on the bed.

Grabbing Dean's hand gently, I interlocked our fingers and my head fell to the floor. I honestly hate crying or showing any emotions whatsoever, but knowing that Dean almost died to protect me is too much for my emotions to hold back. My chest was burning from trying to contain the sobs that started to escape me. My eyes betrayed me once again as tears flowed down my battered face. Everett's arms snaked around my shoulders, and he pulled me back into his chest. His body was warm, and his massive frame encased me in a cocoon. I relaxed into his hold.

I stayed there for a while, holding Dean's hand and resting my body against Everett's, quietly crying as we all looked at Dean, hoping he would wake soon. Just when I thought my body couldn't physically create any more tears, I felt a slight pressure on the hand that was holding Dean's.

"Hey, doll, what are the tears for?" Dean's voice cracked, sounding parched and desperately in need of some water. The audible sigh that came from Everett, Colson, and me was of relief. He was awake and talking. Dean was alive. Being gentle as to not hurt him any further, I lay my body atop of his and embraced all that was Dean. His body was cold and I shivered at the sensation as his arms slowly wrapped around my body.

"How're you feeling?" Everett spoke first, relief in his voice as he approached the bedside and smiled down at his injured brother.

"Like I've been shot, mate."

Colson and I both let out a small chuckle, and the smile that splayed across my face was that of sheer happiness. He was going to be okay. Dean would recover. I rose from his bed, but not before he pulled my head to his and placed his forehead to mine.

"Thank you," I whispered to him as he pulled my head to his lips, pressing a small kiss to my forehead.

"For what?"

"For always protecting me."

"Doll, I need to thank you. If it weren't for you, I'd surely be six feet deep right now." His eyes met mine, and I could only give him a small smile as he released my hand, allowing me to stand.

Just then a knock at the door made me jump and whirl around to see Colson peer over his shoulder at the locked door.

"Fuck, we need to go sweetheart," Colson's expression said this was not up for debate.

CHAPTER 3

SLOAN

I gave Colson a slight nod, and turned back to Dean and Everett. I wrapped my arms around Everett's waist as his arms draped around my body once again.

"See you at home, love. Colson will stay with you until we both get back."

I looked up into his emerald green eyes, a somber look telling me I was safe now. I lifted up tomy tiptoes and gave him a kiss. What I thought was going to be a quick peck on the lips, quickly turned into something more meaningful. His lips were strong and powerful against mine. His kiss spoke words, an apology, a promise, and something else I couldn't decipher.

When he finally released me, he brushed a loose strand of my hair behind my ear and gave me his signature smile. I then turned to Dean and gave him a kiss that was equally, if not more powerful, than

Everett's. If I didn't know any better, I would say they're both trying to compete on whose kiss was better. Boys will be boys. Another knock on the door, but this time louder.

"All right, all right, we have to go now." Colson's eager tone had me rushing to his side.

"You need to put this on again, Sloan. I'm sorry it's not my rule."

I nodded, then turned around so he could fasten the blindfold across my eyes. However, when he was finished, I was still able to see a slight bit beneath the fold with my right eye. Had he done this by accident, or was it intentional?

He turned me toward him and rested his hands on my shoulders. "Okay, sweetheart just like before, stay quiet and I will be your eyes until we reach the car. Sounds good?"

I nodded again, choosing not to speak as he unlocked the door, and I was instantly hit with a chilling breeze from the corridor.

"See you both at home, yeah?" I saw Colson turn towards Everett and Dean, giving them both a nod of agreement.

Colson then intertwined his fingers through mine and started to lead me out the door. I could see a pair of legs standing in the corridor waiting for us to get moving. I could have easily lifted my head to see the identity of the man, but this would have surely told them that this blindfold was not one hundred percent secured. I kept my head down and allowed

Colson to lead the way through whatever this place was.

Leaving the room, we turned left leaving the mysterious man behind us as we quietly made our way down the hall. Turning right at the end of the hall and then another right led us to a flight of stairs.

"Okay, Sloan, there are steps right in front of us, ten to be exact. I will walk slower so you can feel your way to the top."

I nodded as I tilted my head down, giving myself a clear view of the stairs beneath my blindfold. I went slow, trying to make myself look as though I was completely in the dark. He was right; there were exactly ten stairs until we landed at the top and continued straight on.

I found it odd we hadn't passed any additional people. We finally made our way to a door leading us to outside. It was dusk I guessed by the dim lighting that peeked through the blindfold. The air was chilly and so crisp that I couldn't help the deep inhale I took.

I heard the sound of keys jingling and the sound of a car unlocking. I guessed this was Colson, simply because we were still alone as far as I could tell.

"Okay, stop right there, sweetheart. I will help you into the car and once we are out of the compound, I will take off your blindfold."

Again, I nodded and said nothing. His touch was gentle as he grabbed underneath my arm and placed his other hand atop my head so I wouldn't bump it on the frame. Once I was settled in the passenger seat, Colson leaned across me to grab my seatbelt. As he reached the belt, I wrapped my arms around him, squeezing him tight. He didn't miss a beat; he returned the gesture and wrapped me in his arms and squeezed me just as tight. He smelled of rainwater and amber with a hint of sweat. I rested my face in the crook of his neck and inhaled him again, memorizing his scent.

"You scared me, Sloan. I thought we actually lost you." His breath was warm on my ear, and I shivered at the sensation.

"I thought I was lost too."

He pulled away from me so that we were now nose to nose. "I'm never letting you out of my sight again, you hear me?" This was his promise.

I couldn't respond right away, because once his lips were on mine, I was lost to Colson. Tender, sweet, and so incredibly soft, Colson's mouth was hypnotic. He leaned forward, his lips grasping mine, forcing them to part as his tongue invaded my mouth, massaging against mine so slowly, so passionately that I began doing the same. His hand was on the back of my head, keeping our faces locked to one another. A whimper slipped from my throat as our kiss got deeper. I could kiss this man all day. Just as quickly as it had started, it stopped. He pulled away with a sigh and said, "We really have to go now; we are being watched."

With that I sat up straighter and blindly reached

for my seatbelt. Colson helped me click the strap into the buckle and then closed the door behind him.

Moments later he was in the driver's seat, revving the engine and shifting to drive. "As soon as we get out of sight, I will take off your blindfold."

"Okay," was all I could say. We were being watched? By who?

Three minutes later, I felt the car pull to the side of the road and come to a stop.

"Okay I can take the blindfold off now, sweetheart."

He reached over to where I was and gently untied the blindfold. I blinked away the fogginess the blindfold had caused and rubbed my eyes with the palms of my hands. Once I gained my focus, I could see we were parked on the side of a road in the middle of nowhere. There were trees lining the road, but that was all. Just a long, poorly maintained road with no ending and trees hiding us from view.

"Where are we?" I knew this was pointless to ask, so as quickly as I'd asked, I replied,

"Never mind, I know I'm not supposed to know." I looked over at Colson, who was studying me as I examined our surroundings.

"Trust me, I would love to tell you. I hate keeping anything from you, but this secret is bigger than me. Bigger than Everett and Dean. There are several people's lives that depend on the secret of The Shadows. Knowing who we are is already a huge break of rules that I'm sure we'll have consequences for in the future."

We both sat there in silence, allowing the past couple days to sink in. Dean and I had been kidnapped, beaten, tortured, and Dean had been shot. If it weren't for The Shadows, Colson, Everett, and Dean, I would surely be dead or worse—someone's prisoner.

"Who did all this?" My voice was low, almost a whisper. I wanted to know who kidnapped us and who had tried to kill Dean to get to me. How does anybody in Europe know who I am for Christ sakes?

"Van, who was obviously the one who tortured both of you, was able to escape. How? I have no fucking clue, but his days are numbered. We were unable to find anyone else in the warehouse when we went in. They either had a car waiting for them or knew how to use magic and vanish into thin air. We did eliminate some paid security that were positioned around the warehouse, but they were clearly not the ones to orchestrate this whole fuckup."

"So, he or they are still out there?" My voice was shaky.

"Yes, but you have the entire Shadows organization on your side now, so you are safe with us." Colson grabbed my hand, giving it a tight squeeze.

Looking out the window I asked, "Who is trying to kill me, Colson?"

There was a moment of silence in the car. He finally took a deep breath before answering. "We're still not sure yet, sweetheart. But I promise we will find them."

I turned towards him, looking at his beautiful face. I believed him. I trust him, I trust Everett, and Dean. I trust these three men probably more than I should've, since I've only known them for five months.

"Let's go home."

I gave him a small smile and said, "Home."

CHAPTER 4

EVERETT

How could I have let this happen again? Not only did I almost lose Sloan, I almost lost one of my brothers. Sitting in a chair across the room, I looked over at Dean, who was deep in sleep, attached to more wires and tubes than I've ever seen on one person. He looked rough, his skin pale with bruises covering a large portion of his body. He'd taken a serious beating. I couldn't see the burn marks, which would inevitably scar his torso, due to them being covered with bandages, but I knew they were there.

I can feel the heat of anger flash through my face as my body starts to vibrate. I tried to maintain this beast within me.

"You okay, mate? You look like a deranged wolf, and I'm a piece of steak. Don't make me get out of this bed and kick your ass. You know I can," Dean's voice was husky.

I can hear a hint of his asshole sarcasm as he gives me his crooked smile. I gave him a halfhearted smile in return and straightened up my posture, sticking my hands in my trouser pockets to hide the sweat that's started to accumulate.

"I'm fine," is all I can muster. I allowed this pain to happen to him, and I can't bear seeing him lying in this bed looking anything but himself.

"Don't do that to yourself. This isn't your fault. It's no one's fault but the fuckers who did this. You know that, Everett."

Dean has always been able to read my emotions, ever since we were teens. He's what the Shadows call "the observer." He is able to analyze emotions and take in the energy of the room. Thus, allowing him to read people in a way no one else can. I didn't know how to respond. I just stood there, guilt inevitably written all over my face, as Dean stared up at me.

"Where is she now?"

"Colson took her home, along with half a dozen other Shadows that will be strategically placed around the compound for additional protection."

Dean nodded a small gesture, his expression hard and stoic. I could tell he was thinking about something deeply. I'm nowhere as good at reading people as he is, but his eyes give him away.

"What is it?" I asked, not really expecting him to answer me. Dean is not one to express his emotions, not even to Colson or me. He buries a lot of his trauma deep down—in a dark place where no one is allowed entry. So, when he did respond, I was genuinely taken aback.

"I can still hear her screams. Her cries of pure agony are still echoing inside my head."

He paused for a moment, closing his eyes as the images of what they'd gone through danced across his vision. The wrinkles in his forehead give away his pain. He began squeezing his fists into tight balls by his side, and I could feel the anger radiating off him. I could see he was starting to relive in his mind what they'd both gone through—the darkness that some- times consumes him and brings his inner demons to the forefront.

His whole demeanor began changing. His body became stiff, his jaw was tightening, and his breathing fast and chaotic. Just then a beeping sound chimed in from one of the monitors he was currently hooked up to. I looked up to see his blood pressure was slowly rising. He needed to calm down.

"Dean." Trying to get him to open his eyes, I placed my hand atop his shoulder and gave it a small squeeze. "Dean, you're not there anymore, mate. You're here and you're safe. So is Sloan." It took him a minute to slow his breathing to a regular rhythm and finally open his eyes. I gave him a small nod.

I turned and walked back over to the chair I'd been sitting on and pulled it closer to his bed. I took a seat and placed my forearms on my knees, leaning towards the bed. We both were silent for a long while, just allowing the sound of the monitors to echo throughout the room.

"Everett, before I was shot, I heard a familiar voice in the warehouse. Whoever shot me, we know who they are."

I looked up at him, his gaze somewhere far away.

"Wrong move, Dean. He said that right before he pulled the trigger. There was no mistaking it; we know deep inside the fucker who is doing all this."

Dean's tone was full of frustration as he tried to connect the voice with a face. Who the fuck would do this that we know?

"Don't stress yourself out, Dean. We will find out whoever did this, and believe me when I say, this motherfucker will pay. I will personally enjoy filleting his skin off his body for what he did to my family. You have my word."

"Owww! I love it when you talk dirty to me."

CHAPTER 5

SLOAN

I'm not sure when I fell asleep, but the sound of my door opening startled me awake, making me jump in panic.

"It's me, it's just me, Sloan. I'm sorry I scared you." Colson was kneeling beside the car and rested his hand on my thigh. I took a few deep breaths to calm myself and then swung my legs to the side to exit the car. Before I could even stand, Colson swept me into his arms and held me tight to his chest. I could walk and my legs surely weren't broken, but I loved the feeling of his arms encasing me and holding me tight to his body. I nuzzled my face into his neck and gave a small kiss to the sensitive spot just below his ear. He let out a low groan of satisfaction and his body shivered from the touch.

He walked us through the garage and up the stairs

through the door to the house. I threaded my arms around his neck and held on tight as he made his way upstairs and down the hallway. I didn't know where he was taking me, but I didn't care. I was in his arms —safe, protected, and at home.

We reached the room that had been designated as mine and sat me on the edge of the bed. He knelt down between my legs and looked up into my face as his hand found the side of my cheek. I pressed against his touch while he began brushing my cheek with his thumb. This is one of the simplest of gestures but feels the most soothing. All three of the guys have done this simple caress and the feeling of being weightless and loved always fills me up as they cup my face. I'm at their mercy when they do this. I lean into their touch and allow the warmth of their hand to transfer across my face. It's a soothing feeling, a feeling I have yet to experience in my life until I met these three.

"I'm going to start you a bath and help you wash up."

I didn't respond. I just gave him an appreciative smile as he stood up and kissed my forehead before walking to my bathroom and running the tap.

I watched as Colson leaned over the tub and turned on the tap, feeling the running water until the temperature was adequate. He then poured in a few drops of lavender-scented bubble bath. The room quickly filled with the relaxing scent of fresh lavender and a hint of eucalyptus. I inhaled a few deep breaths, closing my eyes and relaxing my head back as the scent filled my nostrils.

I did this for a few more breaths before opening my eyes and seeing Colson removing his long-sleeved shirt, which was covered in grime and what looked to be dark blood stains. I watched him as he raised the shirt above his head, exposing his insanely muscular abdomen and back. His body is unlike any I had ever seen.

Colson has not an ounce of fat on his body. He reminds me of the guys in the fitness magazines that you love to hate because of how defined and lean they are. His muscles pushed against his skin, creating dips and crevices in all the right places. His shaggy blond hair was pulled back into a loose bun, allowing several strands to fall from his elastic and brush across his shoulders. He is a fallen angel, a man created in the form of perfection. He could make any woman weak at the knees with just a glance.

When I look up at Colson, he is looking at me with a cheeky smile splayed across his face. Yes, he just caught me checking him out.

"Come here, Sloan."

I get up from the bed slowly, because now that I have relaxed and the adrenaline of what happened has worn off, a flood of aches and pains shoot through my body, making my face grimace. Damn, I am more beat up than I'd originally thought. Colson noticed my pain and met me halfway to the entrance of the bathroom. He stands directly in front of me, causing me to stop, and he starts slowly and gently removing my clothes so as not to disrupt any of my bandages. He starts with my sweatshirt, grabbing the hem and carefully lifting the ends up my torso. As he does, his fingertips glide across my skin, causing me to shiver—not from cold but from his touch.

He goes slowly, taking into account all the bandages on my arms and shoulders before finally freeing me from my top. I'm not wearing a shirt underneath, so he then transitions to my sweatpants. These are much easier to remove, but he still goes slow, not rushing the act of undressing me. He pulls my pants below my butt, and as he pulls them down my thighs, he start leaving a trail of kisses from my thighs to my knees.

This is Colson, sweet, gentle, and totally in tune with what my body needs. He knows what I've just been through. Even though these boys like to play hard and rough, he knows that's not what I can handle right now. He sparks an electricity inside me with every touch. If Colson had superpowers, which I'm not totally sure he doesn't along with the others, he would have the power to read my body. I never have to tell him what I need, he already knows, some-times even before I do.

"Let's get you in the bath while it's still warm."

I don't hesitate to turn around so he can unlatch my bra. He does so with ease. Then before I can bend down to pull off my panties, he is there looping his fingers and pulling the fabric over my ass. I step out of them one leg after the other.

Turning around so that I'm face to face with Colson, me completely naked and him without a shirt, I can feel the heat of his body radiating off his golden tanned skin. I can't help myself as I lift my hand and place it on his chest. His chest is smooth, not a single strand of hair across his torso. Normally I wouldn't like this in a man; it resembles a teenage boy too much, but on Colson it works. It makes his muscles more profound and chiseled. I rub my hand across his pecs, and he places his hand atop of mine.

"Come on, sweetheart."

He holds my hand and helps me step into the water. The temperature is damn near perfect—hot but not scalding. It's just hot enough so that it turns my skin a slight shade of red. Perfection. I lay back against the cold tub and stretch out my legs. I love this tub. It's one of those really deep ceramic tubs that stands alone with nothing around the edges. I lean my head back, letting Colson grab my hair and lay it on the outside of the tub. He pulls up a stool and sits behind me, his fingers brushing gently through my long hair. Why is it when someone plays with your hair it feels so damn good?

We don't talk for a while. I just lie there, head back, eyes closed, and allow the water to soothe my aching muscles. Colson continues to play with my hair and rub my scalp, giving me the most delicious of massages. His fingers are like magic. With every rub, every scratch he is removing the stress and horrors that have been taking up space in my head for the last twenty-four hours. I don't know when it happens, but I fall asleep as he continues working his magic on me. I'm protected here—in his hands, in this home—and with that I fall into a deep sleep, warm within the tub, being watched over by one of my men.

CHAPTER 6

SLOAN

I'm lying on my stomach on my bed, reading *The Hatchet* by Gary Paulsen, when I hear heavy footsteps coming up the stairs. I had locked my bedroom door, so I continue reading, not thinking too much about whomever it is. Just then my doorknob starts to jiggle, and my father's voice booms through the air.

"Open this fucking door right now, Sloan!" My heart is racing and know without a doubt my father is high or drunk, or shit maybe both. Whenever he is on one of his benders, he becomes angry and violent; hence my locking the door ninety-nine percent of the time.

"I'm not going to say it again, you little bitch! Open this door!"

I know either way if I unlock the door or keep it locked a punishment is inevitable. Most of the time I leave it locked until he gets bored and goes back downstairs to feed his high even more. For some reason I chose to unlock the door, a bad move on my part. I hop off my bed and hurry to the door to unlock the latch. Just when I do, the door swings open, knocking me to the floor.

"Who the fuck do you think you are, locking my door? This is my house, my door, my room; you're just taking up space here!"

I stand back up and fix my clothes, knowing if I respond it won't do me any good. My father steps into my room and starts walking towards me. I only back up a few steps before he grabs me by the arm and yanks me out of the room and down the hall to the bathroom. I've had many punishments from my father in my life. They're usually to strip me down and put me in a freezing cold shower, fill the tub, and hold my head under the water until I am seconds away from blacking out or whipping my ass so bad that I can't sit comfortably for a few weeks. I've prepared myself for these punishments. Sadly, as painful as all these punishments are, I'm no longer afraid, just annoyed.

He squeezes my arm with enough force to leave bruises and pulls me hard into the bathroom we all share. He practically throws me toward the toilet and tells me to sit. I do as I'm told because what's the point in fighting anymore. He tells me to stay put as he leaves the bathroom and goes back down the hall to, I'm guessing, his room. He comes back roughly two minutes later, carrying a rope and puffing on a cigar. This is a new punishment.

My heart starts to thunder as I look at his red, sweaty face and the dazed look in his expression.

"Stand up and put your hands behind your back!"

I hesitate a second too long, and he grabs me by the throat and pulls me to my feet. He then spins me around and pulls my arms behind my back, securing them both together with the scratchy rope. Tying the rope so tight that I know he is cutting off circulation to my hands. He pushes me back to the toilet and tells me to stay still.

"Now you think you can do whatever you want in this house and get away with it? Well, not anymore, Sloan."

Sitting on the toilet seat, I'm genuinely confused, since I've done nothing besides go to school, come home, do my homework, and then had decided to read my book in the confines of my room. I know this is the drugs and alcohol talking, but where the hell does he come up with this shit?

I watch him as he takes a few more puffs of his cigar and blows the smoke into the air. I try hard not to, but the smell of the smoke makes me cough, and this only infuriates him even more.

"What is it? You don't like the smell of my cigar? This Cuban, by the way, I won it with a lucky hand of poker." He was twisting the cigar between his long dirty fingers, smiling as he watched the smoke dance in the air. "Isn't it mesmerizing watching the fire smolder the end of cigars, with every puff the flames burn the tobacco even further down the shaft. I've always enjoyed a good cigar."

He took one deeper inhale and blew out a smoke ring right into my face, causing me to choke and have a coughing fit. My father started laughing, his husky smoker's laugh, deep and raspy echoing in the small room.

"Let's see what happens when the flames meet skin, shall we?" Before I could comprehend what he was talking about, he placed the end of his cigar to my left shoulder. The pain is instantaneous, scorching my skin and melting it away layer by layer. I can't even hear myself scream as the pain engulfs my entire shoulder and radiates down my arm. Just when I think he is about to reach the bone, he lifts his cigar, his laughter becoming audible through the ringing in my ears.

"Please, please, I will never lock my door again!" I cry out, but before I can plead any further, he places the cigar on my arm just below the previous burn. I'm screaming as loud as my lungs will allow, begging and crying for him to stop. I can hear someone saying my name. Ever so faintly, I can hear, "Sloan, Sloan, wake up, please wake up."

I'm thrashing, trying to get the pain of the cigar off my skin and not listening to whomever is calling my name.

"Sloan!! Sloan!!!"

Just then I open my eyes and there's Colson, straddling me in the tub with both hands on my shoulders shaking me. He's still in his jeans, which are completely soaked from my thrashing. My breathing is erratic and wild. Water coats the bathroom floor.

"Look at me, Sloan, look at me!" His voice is loud as he tries to get my attention and bring me back from a terrible memory. I feel lost in my subconscious.

"It's just a dream, sweetheart, you're only dreaming."

I finally find Colson's green eyes, green with a hint of hazel all swirled into two gorgeous irises. He releases my shoulders and cups my face with both of his hands, holding my head still as I slowly steady my breathing.

"Are you OK? You were just dreaming." His face was full of worry, his forehead furrowed and his mouth slightly ajar as if he, too, were breathing heavily. I squeeze my eyes shut to stop the sting of tears from escaping.

"Sloan," is all he kept saying.

I fall apart. I fucking hate crying in front of the guys, or anyone for that matter, but the sobs that come from my mouth are those of a tortured soul. My chest is heaving, as pained cries slip between my lips. Colson submerges himself even further into the tub and pulls me into his lap. I am now straddling him as his arms wrap around my wet body. Our chests are pressed tightly against each other. I wrap my arms around his neck and rest my face on his shoulder as tears, drool, and water escape from me. Attractive, Sloan, real attractive.

For years, I have forgotten this memory of what my father did to me, in order to suppress the pain and torment he caused me. I can't remember the last time I recollected this time in my life in such extensive detail. I don't know why I have done so now, except maybe it has to do with the trauma Dean and I had just experienced, not even a full twenty-four hours ago.

Colson traces shapes along my back and lets me cry, allowing me to release all the emotion I have been locking up inside myself. It was only a matter of time until it all boiled over and exploded like a ticking time bomb. Out of all the guys, I'm glad it was Colson who saw this and not the others. Colson cares for me in the moment, not allowing his mind to wander anywhere else. He simply sees my pain and reacts to try and soothe my pain. Dean and Everett immediately go into protector mode. They want to know who caused my pain, what happened, and how they are going to kill them. They mean well, yes, but Colson knows how to handle emotion first and then kill the tormentor later.

We sit in the tub together wrapped in each other's embrace until I feel like my body can produce no more tears. I lean back away from his chest and all I can do is stare at him. His beautiful features—his pink, plump lips, high cheekbones, and those eyes that are so beautifully unique I could get lost in them.

He lifts his hand and wipes away the few remaining tears on my cheeks before saying,

"Sweetheart, are you okay?"

I sniffle, very pathetically I might say, before I say, "Yes, I'm sorry I didn't mean to unload all that on you."

His smile stretches across his face. "You never have to apologize to me, Sloan, you need to let that out. You're by far the strongest woman I've ever met, but we all need to let go of emotions once in a while. Honestly from what you've been through in the past few days, this was way past due."

I give him a weak smile before leaning forward and kissing him, thanking him with affection rather than meaningless words. He kisses me back, snaking his arms around my back and pulling me into him once again.

"Are we interrupting something?" A familiar voice fills the air.

I lean back from our kiss, startled to hear that someone else is here. When I look to see who it is, my body relaxes again. They're both here.

"Dean, Everett, you're home."

CHAPTER 7

SLOAN

Everett is in the doorway to the bathroom with a smug smile drawn on his face. His arms are crossed, and he's leaning against the doorframe as if he'd been observing us for a while. He's wearing his usual dark jeans and a V-neck black shirt that displays a large portion of his tattoos that are beautifully painted across his pecs.

Dean is to his right, standing so stoically as if he hadn't been shot and tortured. His face is somber yet hiding something that I can't put my finger on. His hands are in his gray sweatpants' pockets, and he's wearing a black loose sweatshirt. His face still displays his battle wounds, a war zone of black, blue, and purplish bruises covering most of his handsome face. I immediately shut down my mind as it starts to go back to the warehouse and hear his screams echo throughout the hollow area. I clench my jaw at the thought of him being in such agony.

I jump out of the tub and quickly wrap a towel around my soaked naked body before embracing Dean. He doesn't hesitate returning the favor, because just as I wrap my arms around his waist, his long arms have already interlocked around my lower back. He's bent over, since, damn, he's tall; he's definitely the tallest out of the three. I fear my hugging him, or him just bending over, is causing him pain, but if it does, he doesn't show it. His embrace is strong, not tight where it hurts but strong enough where he shows me he was truly worried for my well-being, as I was for his. I rest my head against his chest, feeling the thunder of his heartbeat.

"I thought I'd lost you." My voice comes out as a shaky whisper.

It takes a moment for him to respond, as we continue to stay wrapped up in each other's warmth.

"I thought the same about you." His voice is husky and raspy at the same time, but clearer than when we were at the hospital, or whatever that place was.

I hear behind me the sound of sloshing water and loud splashes, which leads me to assume Colson has made his way out of the tub as well.

"Thanks for the interruption, mate," Colson says, and I smile into Dean's chest.

"She needs to rest. I told you to make sure she

relaxes as soon as she gets home." Everett's tone is not harsh, but there is a hint of seriousness as he addresses Colson.

"She fell asleep in the tub and started having a nightmare. Why do you think I was half clothed in there? If we were messing around, I definitely wouldn't still have my trousers on, now, would I?"

He had a point there. Everett didn't ask any more questions but turned to look at me with his piercing blue eyes. He didn't have to say a word; his eyes did all the talking for him.

"It was nothing really, just a past memory stamped in my mind. Really, I'm fine." I looked over at Colson who's studying me intently. I give him a "leave it alone" look, and as if he is reading my mind, he does just that.

I back up from Dean's embrace and give Everett a hug next. He brushes my wet hair back with one of his hands, then places his lips to the top of my head. His body is so warm, so deliciously comforting, it's hard to let go. Once I do, I step back and admire the three of them.

Their beautiful faces are all uniquely attractive in their own ways. They each have a look of worry etched across their faces. Worry for my well-being, my mental state, or my fresh marks that will now join the plethora of scars that already pepper my body. Their gazes start to become too much.

"Please, stop looking at me as if I'm a damaged

little girl who might combust into flames at any moment."

I can't look at them in the face as I speak. I know what they all must think of me. Here's an American girl who lived a pitiful, brutal life; who is forever attracting danger and horrors at every turn. Yes, I've lived through hell and back. A life that I would never wish upon my worst enemy, but I refuse to be labeled as a broken woman. I may have been through a lot, but I've fought tooth and nail to become my own person, my own savior. I will not be seen as the victim any longer.

After last night at the warehouse and my endless nightmares of my piece of shit father, I'll no longer allow the darkness to cripple me anymore. I'm Sloan, I've survived this long and fuck if I'm going to let another man try and steal anything more from me.

"You are far from a damaged little girl, Sloan." Dean made his way towards me in one long stride.

Pulling his hands from his pockets he cupped my chin and tilted it up so that we're now standing face to face.

"I've seen firsthand how insanely fucking strong you are, and for anyone to think you are anything but a fierce warrior has no fucking clue what you're capable of. You're more than just a person who's been through some dark shit, Sloan. What I saw in that warehouse was a true fighter, and someone who saved my life that would have surely been lost if you weren't there. So, don't ever think we see you as damaged; if anything, we see someone who is capable of protecting herself. But know this, you won't have to fight this evil alone. You're with us now, ours, and a part of this family as much as the three of us are brothers."

He leaned down and kissed my lips in such a way that made me feel like his words were more than words, but a promise. A promise that has bound us together forever.

His words penetrate straight to my core. I closed my eyes as I let his confession fully consume me. Never has anyone referred to me as a warrior, nor has anyone ever called me theirs. A few months ago, if someone were to tell me I would be in this position with these three men, I would have thought they were out of their damn minds. But now, standing between the three of them, I can't imagine what my life could have been if they hadn't come for me—or what would have become of me if they hadn't gone back to Stone Fortress to retrieve me. It's funny how the world works, isn't it?

"Come on, doll, you need to rest." Dean scoops me up in his arms and begins carrying me to my bed.

"Put me down. You're hurt and you shouldn't be lifting anything!" I yell at him. I don't mistake the sly smile that comes across his face as he gently lowers me down.

"Don't bitch and moan, mate, when you tear open

your stitches," Colson says from the bathroom entrance. I give Dean a look of agreeance as he stands back up, looking unfazed by any of our bickering. I know he is in pain from his wounds, but damn does he do a good job at hiding it.

"You need to rest, Sloan; you've been through a lot and what your body needs most is sleep."

Dean is right, I do need rest, but now that they are all back home, I don't want to be left alone. In fact, I don't want to go to sleep. Who knows what horrible dreams await me there? I sit on my bed, wrapped in my towel, and watch as Everett and Colson enter the room.

"He's right, love, you need your rest so your body can heal properly." Everett looks down at me as he makes his way over to stand in front of me.

"I don't need to sleep, I'm fine." I know I am being a pretentious little brat by denying what my body needs, but I am honestly too afraid to close my eyes right now. All I want is to be wherever they are.

"Let me rephrase that, you and Dean both need to rest. You've both been through a lot; there's no denying that. As much as I want to be the one to sleep in your bed, why don't you and Dean get some rest together and we will reconvene in the morning," Everett's tone is non-negotiable. I look at Dean who looks annoyed that he is being told what to do, but also accepting that he gets to share my bed with me.

"Lucky bastard," Colson mutters under his breath.

I'm not sure he wanted anyone to hear his comment, but I smile at his banter.

Dean and I both nod at each other, and he begins to remove his sweatshirt, exposing his bandaged chest and making it hard for me to look away. His torso is covered with white, thick bandages covering his wounds. I don't miss the slight hint of pink on the bandage covering his gunshot wound.

"Stubborn bastard, I knew he would tear his stitches." I hear Colson say as he begins opening and closing my dresser drawers, retrieving an oversized shirt and a pair of panties. He brings both over to me.

"Here ya go, sweetheart, let me help you get into these. You'll be more comfortable than wearing a damp towel."

I give him an appreciative smile and drop the towel from around my body. He slowly helps me thread my arms through the shirt and then bends down to do the same with my panties. One foot and then next, he slides the fabric up my calves and then my thighs. I stand to allow him to pull the panties over my ass.

Once I'm dressed, he keeps his hands on my hips and gives me a searing kiss that has my legs falling weak.

"Sleep well, sweetheart."

He reluctantly pulls back from me, and I hate the feeling of his lips leaving mine. I look over my shoulder and see that Dean has already made his way into bed, pulling the covers over his legs and resting his arms above his head. I turned to Everett, who had taken the spot Colson just left. Wrapping his arms around my waist, he bends down to the crook of my neck, kissing me and sending shivers throughout my body. Damn, these boys are irresistible. What have they done to me?

"If you need me, I'm just right outside the door." His tone is low, only audible enough for him and me to hear.

He pulls his face away from my neck and cups my face with one of his hands. His bright blue eyes see right through to my soul. He sees me, all of me. Pulling my face to his, he kisses me, his lips like fire melting into my mouth as he continues to hold me to him. This moment is more than just a kiss between the two of us; it feels more like worry or an apology. Maybe from all that has happened, he feels responsible somehow. I wrap my arms around his neck and hold him tight, hoping that this gesture tells him that I don't blame him, not at all. If anything, I'm thankful. If they hadn't come, Dean and I would be dead. No doubt about it.

Our lips unlock and he rests his forehead to mine, our gaze hard on one another.

"Thank you, Everett, thank you for everything."

His weak smile is barely noticeable, guilt lacing his expression instead. He pulls back from me.

"Get some rest, you two, and if you need us, we will be right outside."

Dean gives a salute to Everett as I watch him exit

the bedroom, but before he closes the door fully, he turns his head over his shoulder and says, "I'm sorry this happened to you both. I would never forgive myself if I lost either of you." With that he closes the door gently, and I listen as his footsteps fade away down the hall.

CHAPTER 8

DEAN

She stands in the middle of the room staring at the door Everett just left from. Her small frame being swallowed up by her oversized shirt. It's one of my simple black tees she stole from my room a few weeks ago. I can't hide the twitch in my cock at the sight of her in my clothes.

Her exposed legs stand utterly still as Everett's footsteps become a faint sound as he makes his way down the hall. She stands there a bit longer, staring at the closed door before turning around and stealing my soul with her diamond-blue eyes cutting deep into my chest. Her eyes tell a dark, haunting story that only she holds the key to. There is no denying she's lived a tough life, as did the rest of us, but her story is unique. Where we continued to live in the darkness of a turbulent life, she fought like hell and escaped a life that could have killed her, slowly. She is stronger than the three of us in that sense. The only reason she's found herself back into the clutching hands of darkness is because of us.

"Come here, Sloan."

She obeys making her way over to the opposite side of the bed. She pulls the covers down, sliding one leg underneath and then the other.

I'm resting my back against the headboard, my arms interlocked behind my head. She does the same resting her back against the cushions of the headboard, and pulls the covers over her waist before turning to look at me.

"Can we stay up for a bit, please? I'm not really tired. We could watch TV or something."

"You're an adult, Sloan, you don't need my permission to stay up late." I don't miss the small chuckle that escapes her perfect mouth, and it's a comforting sound.

She looks away from me and around the room, no doubt looking for the remote for the TV that's mounted on her wall.

"Looking for this?" I say, holding the remote that I retrieved from the nightstand the moment I got in bed. Like hell was I going right to bed like Daddy Everett wanted us to do. I teasingly waved the remote back and forth, as she turns and sees what I'm holding.

"I'm glad to see your gunshot wound hasn't

altered your personality in any way." She reaches for the remote, and I pull it away, taunting and teasing her more. She starts making her way closer and closer to me, trying to grab the remote, just as I wanted.

"Come on, hand it over, damn it." She's not mad, but her slight frustration makes me smile at her. It's cute that she thinks she can win against me, since I'm more than double, maybe even triple her size.

"I need something first then you can have it and watch whatever you American girls watch."

She narrows her eyes at me, but stills with curiosity. "What?" she says hesitantly as she tilts her head like a curious puppy. She braces herself for whatever it is I'm about to say. I can visually see her shoulder tense.

"I want to know why you risked your life protecting me in the warehouse? Why protect one of the men that ultimately caused you to be in that situation in the first place? Why not run and protect yourself?" My tone is cold and serious, not mean in a way where I'm not thankful she didn't put her life on the line for me, but genuinely curious why she felt she had to.

She sits back against the headboard, silent, as she continues to stare at me with those fucking hypnotic eyes of hers. There is a long moment where neither of us speak a word, and the tension in the room begins to weigh on me. I'm about to say never mind, when she answers my question.

"Because, even though I'm here because of you three, I have never felt like I've belonged anywhere. When I'm with you, Everett, and Colson, there is a feeling of completeness or wholeness, rather, that has forever been empty for me. You've all protected me many times within the last five months when you didn't have to. You've fought, beaten, and God knows what else to ensure my safety, and for that I owe you guys everything. You easily could have left me at Stone Fortress, finishing your job by dropping me off and thought no more of me, but you didn't. Plus, it's more than me owing you guys; I care for you. I care for the three of you and hope your feelings are the same."

She looked down at her hands, studying them as if looking for something she's lost. Again, we sat in silence for a moment, the words between us being so raw, so honest, and so much more than I was expecting. She's so fucking brave, so smart, and so beautiful I have to admit my feelings are much stronger than just caring for her. Looking at her now, I want nothing more than to fucking destroy everyone who's hurt her in the past. I want to protect her because little does she know, she's mine, she's ours, now and forever.

I cup her chin and turn her face to mine. Narrowing my eyes on her, I say,

"There will be times when one of us is in danger, there always is when it comes to this job, but I need you to promise me, promise us, you will never try to sacrifice yourself for us. You survive. That's your job, Sloan. You survive."

She looked at me with concern, and confusion blanketed across her face before pulling her face away from my grasp.

"So, you wanted me to let you die in that warehouse, is that what you're saying?"

"No one ever wants to die, darling. I just need you to know your life is more precious than either one of ours. You're a fighter, so you fight for your life and survive."

She doesn't respond. She looks at me as though I just grew three heads before dropping her head down once again and ponders my words. She inhales deeply before saying, "I can't make that promise, Dean. You all mean too much to me now, and if something were to happen to either of you, something I might be able to prevent, I couldn't forgive myself."

I'm about to interrupt her before she speaks again.

"Let me finish. The situation we are in is complicated, and if one of us is in danger, then we all are. So, fuck if I'm going to just roll over and die. I've never done that in my life, and I'll be damned if I do that now. You're going to have to deal with that."

I can't help the deep sense of pride that I feel in my chest as she speaks. I've never met a person, better yet a woman, who can match my energy, but damn if this woman isn't a replica of me in female form. So, I give in.

"Fine," is all I say in response.

"Fine? That's it, just fine?" She's looking at the side of my face as I turn on the TV and start flipping mindlessly through the channels.

"What do you want me to say? Beg you not to fight, not to be the warrior you already are. Anything I say won't change who you are, Sloan, and I don't want you to change. You've seen what happens when we fight back. It's dirty, painful, and, truthfully, fucking hell. You've seen it and experienced it first-hand, yourself. As much as I don't want anything to happen to you, I can't force you to do anything. You're not a caged animal, Sloan; you're a fucking wolf. You're loyal to a fault and possess a fierceness I've never seen before. You survive. You've proven that already, and you protect those around you whom you care for. I can't and I won't ask you to change because your strength is admirable and it keeps you alive. Just know if anything ever happens to you, the earth itself will split in half, unleashing the devil himself upon the poor soul who is responsible."

The room falls quiet except for the background sounds of the TV. I slide my back down the headboard and settle in for the night, watching whatever the fuck this reality show is that I've landed on. A half second later Sloan does the same, sliding closer to me until our bodies are touching and her hand gently lays across my chest.

We lay there for a while until I feel her breathing even out and she slowly slips into sleep. Her warm hand still draped across my chest flinches just slightly as her body relaxes. I wrap my arm around her and allow myself to follow her into the darkness of sleep. Two broken souls intertwined as one while the horrors of our nightmares flood our minds.

CHAPTER 9

SLOAN

My dreams are filled with my usual horrors of my past but are now joined with a large warehouse and endless screaming from myself and a single gunshot that startles me awake with a violent jerk. Sitting straight up in bed, I look to my side and notice Dean is gone. It doesn't take me long to find him, the steam blooming out of the bathroom indicates he is taking a rather scalding shower. The room is still dark with just a hint of the morning sun starting to rise outside. I pull my legs to my chest and allow myself a moment to catch my breath before standing and making my way to the bathroom.

As I stand in the doorway, it takes my eyes a moment to see through the thick cloud of steam, and realize the person standing beneath the stream of water is not Dean at all; it's Everett. His back is facing me, allowing a perfect view of his insanely toned ass.

I lean against the doorframe, not wanting to disturb him but also wanting to watch like the pervert I've become since being around these men. They are all so beautiful.

"You like the view? Why don't you join me?" His voice startles me out of my trance. He's still facing away from me. How does he know I'm watching? I swear he has eyes in the back of his head or something. He brushes his hands through his hair, and I watch the flow of water cascade down his back.

He didn't have to ask me twice. I saunter my way over to the shower as I discard my nightshirt, or rather Dean's shirt, and strip off my panties. Opening the large glass door, I hesitate a moment as steam billows out, warming my body while it dances around my frame. As the steam dissipates, my eyes adjust to the most beautiful view. Everett stands there, water flowing over every dip and curve of his muscular body, a devilish smirk on his face as he reaches his hand out to mine.

"That didn't take too much convincing to get you here."

"The shower is turning into our 'thing,' don't you think?" I say, stepping into the spray of the shower.

"That it is, my dear."

Once I'm fully in the shower, Everett pulls me in close, wrapping his long, muscular arms around me. We stand there for a long while savoring the feeling of our bodies pressed against one another. Moments like these are just one of the many reasons why I adore this man. His mere presence and touch bring me to a state of euphoria that allows me to forget about the world around me and just become lost in his embrace.

"How're you feeling today, love?"

As he speaks his chest vibrates with every word against my cheek that's rested upon his chest. With one hand wrapped around my lower back, his other hand starts massaging my scalp.

"I'm fine." Lie, this was an utter lie. Honestly, I didn't know how I was feeling. The only thing making me feel better was the fact that I was back here, in their home, with all three of them with me.

"Don't lie to me."

I inhaled deeply, trying to not suck in water in the process, and I stepped out of his hold. Looking at his beautiful face, I knew he wouldn't believe me when I said I was fine, but hell it was worth a shot.

"Honestly, I don't know how I feel. How's one supposed to feel, really? All I know is I'm happy we are all alive, safe, and here together."

Are we safe, though? I wasn't too sure. His hand reached my cheek, and his thumb brushed along my lower lip ever so softly. I closed my eyes to his touch, letting my face relax into his palm.

"I'm so sorry, Sloan. I shouldn't have suggested we go on that ride. I've put you in more danger, and for that I almost lost you and a brother," His voice was pained, and guilt plastered his face as he spoke. "I fucked up. I—"

"Enough with the apologies, Everett. Guilt is not a good look on you. This is no one's fault. You told me earlier I was free to go whenever I wanted to. I chose to stay. I could have easily left and flew back to the States but I didn't. I'm here and in this, just as much as you three. This isn't the first time I've been kidnapped, and it probably won't be the last."

There was a long pause between us, his expression going dark beneath the water trickling down his face.

"That's where you're wrong. That was the last time, and when I said you were free to go, I lied. You're with us now, our girl, my girl. You're not going anywhere. I don't want you to leave, and I have a strong feeling neither do you." His eyes darkened with every word he spoke.

I hadn't noticed until my back touched the cold tile of the shower, but he was closing the short space between us, and I had to crane my neck to see his face.

"You were mine the moment you ran into me at Stone Fortress. You were mine the moment our lips touched. You were mine all along and just never knew it. So, yes, love, I am sorry and will continue to apologize to you because no man should ever put his woman in harm's way."

His lips crashed into mine with such force, I had no doubt that in this moment I was surely his, and that's exactly what I wanted to be.

Out of all three guys, Everett has a way of making me feel as though I've been a part of this world my whole life. He's protective and nurturing, but above all else he will do just about anything to protect me from any and all dangers that will surely find me again. But the question I have is why? Why is this man so willing to risk his life and those of his brothers to protect me? I'm nobody, just a stray from Florida for all he knows. I'm nothing special, yet these men are ready to jump in front of a bullet for me. I know they feel guilty for ultimately putting me in this situation, but clearly there has to be something else I'm missing. Why am I so special? I needed answers, but right now I needed him more.

I wrapped my hands around his neck and pulled him in tight as our tongues continued to explore one another's mouths. Our hot, wet bodies were pressed so firmly together I could feel his ever-growing erection pressing into my stomach. The spray of the shower wasn't doing anything to hide the slickness that was building between my legs. Everett placed one hand around my neck, applying just the right amount of pressure that balanced on the edge of pain and pleasure. I never knew someone's hands could be my new favorite accessory, but the way his hands fit ever so perfectly around my neck had my stomach fluttering and my pussy throbbing.

His other hand slowly swept down my chest, caressing my breasts before sliding lower down my stomach and finding the bundle of nerves between my legs. His fingers were that of a musician, playing me and working me up to a climax in record time.

"Don't come yet, love. Wait until I'm inside of you."

A breathing moan escaped my mouth as our tongues continued to fight one another. I was so close already; I couldn't hold off for much longer. As if he read my mind, he removed his fingers from my clit, and I bucked my hips in protest.

"Don't stop, please don't stop," I begged. He pulled back from our kiss, looking down at me with a devilish grin.

"You'll come when I'm ready for you to come." With no warning, he thrusted so hard inside me, the pain of his entrance was soon forgotten when his grip on my throat tightened just a little more causing the pleasure of his dick inside me to feel euphoric. He pulled out slowly until just the tip of him was inside me, and then thrusted hard again.

He continued doing this as his grip on my throat never let up. I was still holding on to his neck for dear life as he fucked me like a possessive alpha claiming what was his. His mouth found my collarbone, sucking and biting as his thrust picked up speed.

"Your pussy is fucking perfect, and it's all mine."

I could have melted right then, and I surely would have if he wasn't holding me up by my neck. I could feel my climax building with every thrust, with every bite and suck of his mouth.

"I'm about to come, I'm coming!" I couldn't hold back any longer. With my warning, Everett sped up even faster slamming me harder against the tile. I hitched one leg up around his waist, pulling him into me as my climax hit me like a tsunami crashing through me. As I shuddered and trembled through my pleasure, his hold on my neck eased up making my climax that much stronger. His orgasm following mine as he pushed himself so deep inside me, I could feel his hot cum fill me up.

He wasn't done just yet; he grabbed my jaw with his hand, pulling me into his kiss as his other hand found my swollen clit. He began slowly massaging as his cum began sliding down my leg.

"You're the most addicting drug I've ever had. The way I want you even more with just a simple moan from your perfect mouth is a dangerous superpower." His voice was low and husky as he slowly came down from his high, giving me butterflies.

"I could say the same about you with your fingers and what they do to me." Replying in almost a whisper, I tried to catch my breath. He let out a small laugh as he pressed gentle kisses along the length of my neck.

After incredible morning sex, we began washing up with the floral-scented shampoos and soap, leaving the room filled with a delicious aroma. As we both finished and stepped out of the shower, Everett grabbed the large, white, fluffy robe and draped it around my shoulders. He found his towel and wrapped it around his waist, exposing his delicious *V*. I blurted out,

"Why am I so special to you? Why are you so keen on protecting me?"

He didn't respond right away. He just wiped the condensation from the mirror and looked at me through the reflection. His face was stoic. He looked as though he was battling his inner thoughts on whether he wanted to tell me or not. I walked up behind him and wrapped my arms around his waist and rested my hands on his chest. He let out a sigh before responding.

"Sloan, do you know who you are…?"

CHAPTER 10

SLOAN

"What do you mean, do I know who I am? I'm Sloan, an American girl who grew up in a shitty household and escaped the moment I could. What else is there to know?" I dropped my hands from his chest and backed up so I could see his face more clearly. "What do you mean, Everett?" I said again when he didn't respond right away. His gaze never faltered from mine. He still didn't respond as my temper started to rise. "Everett, for fuck's sakes, tell me."

Just as he was about to answer, the bedroom door swung open, and Colson came barreling into the bathroom.

"Good morning, sweetheart!" Colson's muscular arms snaked around my waist, and he lifted me into a hug, spinning me around a few times before placing me back down on the cool tile. Leaning down, he kissed my lips before looking up and noticing Everett was also in the bathroom.

"Morning, mate, I see you got dibs on our girl this morning. Can't say that I'm not jealous."

Colson always could make me smile with his childish commentary, but I hadn't forgotten my conversation with Everett. Colson felt the tension in the room, looking between the both of us he said, "Am I missing something? Why does it look like you're in the bloody doghouse, bro?" Colson gave me a wink and looked back to Everett, waiting for his response.

"Everett was just about to tell me a little bit more about myself that I don't already know."

Colson's smile instantly faded from his handsome face as he glared daggers at Everett.

"She's going to find out sooner or later; better tell her now so she's prepared," Everett finally spoke up, responding to Colson.

"We don't know all the details, mate. Plus, we said we would wait and tell her when we were all together."

"Excuse me, but does everyone know except me? And stop talking as if I'm not in the room." My temper was quickly coming to the surface. There was a long pause as I watched the guys stare off in a silent battle between one another. Just as I was about to explode, a voice chimed in from behind me.

"Why don't you both get dressed and meet Colson and me downstairs? It looks like we've got some shit to discuss." Dean's husky voice had my head turning towards him. He was standing in the doorway, looking fresh from a shower, water still glistening in his hair. He was in his gray sweatpants and a black V-neck T-shirt. Looking at him now, you would never think he'd been recently shot and tortured.

I walked across the bathroom to him and hugged him gently so as not to hurt his wounds. He hugged me but then pulled back to softly kiss my forehead. Why was this so fucking attractive to us women? It's such a small gesture, yet it leaves me feeling like jelly in his hands.

"Get dressed little one, we will fill you in." He looked up from my face, glancing from Colson to Everett.

"I'll be in the kitchen; come on, Colson." He turned and left the room with Colson in tow. Once they were gone, I turned back to Everett.

"Why do I feel like this news is going to hurt?"

He didn't hesitate even for a second. Everett took two long strides before cupping my face in his hands. "No matter what, you have the three of us. Like I said before, you're with us now."

We both got dressed in comfy clothes, since I doubted we were leaving the house today, and made our way down to the kitchen where the guys were waiting.

The sweet aroma of freshly made coffee filled the space, and I inhaled deeply, allowing the smell to invade my senses. Coffee always put a dopey smile on my face, no matter what mood I was currently in. Coffee could always be counted on to bring me happiness. Walking into the kitchen, I was met with a mug of steaming hot coffee, brought to me by an even hotter shirtless man.

"Why thank you, Colson, but where is your shirt?" Not that I was complaining seeing his half-naked body.

"Ditched it. I was getting a little overheated after seeing you in that robe." He gave a mischievous smirk as he handed me my coffee. I could get used to this every morning.

"Thank you." I reached up on my tiptoes and kissed his cheek before making my way to a stool at the island. Sitting down, I took a small sip of my coffee, allowing the burn to heat me up as I swallowed it down with a satisfying moan.

The kitchen was quiet as Everett poured himself a cup of coffee, and Colson jumped up to sit on the counter, sipping from his own mug. Dean was leaning against the counter opposite of me, with his arms folded across his chest. No one spoke for a good while. We all enjoyed our coffee except for Dean. My curiosity soon got the best of me and I blurted out, "So, you guys have something to tell me?" Resting my elbows on the island, I looked between the three of them, seeing which one would speak first. It was clear by looking at Dean and Colson, who were both looking at Everett, that they were waiting for him to break the ice.

I looked at Everett as well while he held my gaze for what seemed like an eternity before finally speaking. "Sloan, tell me what you know about your family? Specifically, your father's side of your family."

Giving him a curious look, I wasn't expecting that question. I sat for a moment, trying to remember the only time I had met anyone from my father's side of the family.

"I've never met anyone besides my grandfather. Well, I technically didn't meet him, just saw him for a moment. I can't even tell you his name. I just remember he was a very tall man, with dark hair and an accent I couldn't pinpoint from where. He wore a black suit and came with a couple of his friends that were equally as tall and wore suits as well. They stayed outside, though they never came into the house. It was so brief. I was ten years old, and he randomly showed up at our house and only spoke to my father. I was told to go to my room and stay there, but I snuck out and started eavesdropping from the hallway. They were arguing, my father and him, about stepping up and taking his spot in the family, or something along those lines."

My father was so far gone at this time with drugs, it was like arguing with a brick wall. Trying to remember what was said between the two of them, I looked between the guys, each one listening so intently.

"Anything else you remember about that argument?" Everett asked.

I sat back in my stool, closing my eyes. I tried to go back to that day so many years ago.

"My father kept shouting at him about never being a part of his family again. My grandfather said something about wanting to meet his granddaughter, but my father shut that down instantly. The last thing I remember my grandfather saying was he would meet me one day and how my father didn't deserve me. He also mentioned how my father was a disappointment to his name."

The kitchen was in total silence as Everett, Dean, and Colson looked among one another, worry etched in their faces.

"What?" I said impatiently.

"What's your last name, Sloan?"

I furrowed my eyebrows. Looking at Everett, I said, "Uhm, it's Wallace. Why?" Everett gave another look to Colson and Dean as if needing confirmation about what he was about to say.

"When we discovered that people were hunting you, we had one of the techs at headquarters look into your past more closely. We didn't understand why our job was to simply kidnap you and essentially deliver you to Osiris." Everett paused a moment before continuing.

"They found a connection between your father and a man named Shem Wallace. We learned that Shem is your grandfather's first name." Everett stopped talking and gave me a second to comprehend what he'd just said.

"Okay, so what makes that such a secret that needed to be kept from me?"

"Because, Sloan, Shem Wallace is currently the head of the Irish mob." Everett's tone was sharp.

The Irish fucking mob! This is a joke. These guys are messing with me. There is no way my drug addicted, deadbeat, alcoholic man of a father could be the son of a kingpin, making me his granddaughter. My mind was racing a million miles a minute. Looking down at my coffee, I noticed my hands were trembling, making my coffee swirl in my mug. Trying to wrap my head around this new family drama, Dean broke my racing thoughts by saying, "This makes you the granddaughter of the most powerful organized crime group in all of Europe."

I looked at him with worry and concern plastered across my face.

"With this information in the hands of the wrong people, let's say the enemies of your grandfather could possibly want you dead," Colson said matter-of-factly.

"Or kidnap you for leverage against your grandfather," Everett spoke up as he lifted his mug to his lips.

"Leverage for what?" My voice was quivering.

"Anything really—money, power, territory—whatever it is Shem possesses that is desired," Dean answered.

"Jesus Christ, I *am* living in a Liam Neeson movie. This isn't real. Shit like this doesn't happen, right?" I said to no one in particular.

"Happens in our world, unfortunately," Colson said under his breath. This comment was met with a punch to his thigh from Everett.

"Fuck, mate what was that for?" Everett didn't answer; he just glared death at Colson which got the message across.

I sat there, sipping my coffee and looking into my mug as if the answers to my questions were floating around the dark liquid. The guys let me sit there in silence for a moment, allowing this all to sink in.

"So, what do we do now?" I finally said, not looking up from my mug? I heard someone walking but didn't bother looking up to see who it was. A pair of strong hands wrapped around my waist and spun my stool around to face them.

"Now, you leave it to us. We will figure out who is trying to take you from us." Everett's tone was laced with death. I had no doubt that he and the guys would find the assholes behind all this. But like hell was I just going to sit back and let them do all the work. This is my twisted fucked-up life, and I was not going to let the control of others continue to write my story. It was mine to create and mine to live. Enough of this damsel in distress bullshit; it's time to toughen the hell up and start doing more to protect myself.

As much as I enjoyed and appreciated the guys always protecting me, I need to do my part and prove to whomever was after me that I am not the one to fuck with anymore.

"As much as I appreciate you guys wanting to protect me all the time, I'm not just going to sit back and let you do all the work. I want to help; it's my life and my supposed family, so I want to be just as involved as you three." My gaze wandered between the three of them. Each one looked worried in their own way.

"No, I'm not putting you in any more danger, Sloan. I've fucked up enough these past few months, and I'm not doing it again. You need to do exactly as I say to ensure your safety. That's my top priority, your safety."

"You can't just tell me what to do. I'm not a child, Everett. This shit has everything to do with me, and I will be damned if I just sit back and do nothing." I raised my voice in anger. Who the hell did he think he was telling me what to do?

"I will not let anyone else touch, hurt, or take you again, and if that means I have to put you on house arrest, so be it." Everett's face was set in a hard line, and he was not giving me any hints of budging on this matter, but I was not giving up.

This was the controlling Everett, the possessive alpha male coming out to play this morning, but I had my own alpha personality as well—and she was ready to fight.

I stood up from my stool to face him properly. "I'm not some animal you can keep in a cage!" I poked Everett's chest with my finger, causing him to tense his muscles as I continued to press him. I could tell he was getting irritated with my disobedience, but I could give a fuck.

"You just told me my grandfather is the leader of the Irish freaking mob, and you expect me to sit here and get lost in my thoughts while the three of you go out and play spy, trying to find the assholes who are trying to kidnap me?" I was poking him harder with each word I spoke. The tension in the room grew as I raised my voice higher.

As I stood on my tiptoes to get in his face, Everett snatched my hand with his, stopping me from poking him again. He made himself taller and stepped into me, causing me to look up at him due to his towering height.

"Poke me again, and I will tie you up. Is that what you want?"

My cheeks pinked, because honestly that didn't sound like a punishment to me, but in his context, I don't think it was meant to be the *fun* kind of tied up.

"You wouldn't dare?"

"Try me, love." His body vibrated with anger as his grip on my wrist tightly. We stared off with one another before Colson broke our silent battle.

"All right, let's all just take a fucking chill pill, shall we? We can discuss the matter of imprisonment of our girl later, Everett. Right now, can we just enjoy a nice family breakfast?" Colson winked at me as I ripped my wrist from Everett's grasp and sat my ass back on the stool.

Colson waited until I sat down before saying, "So, who wants waffles?" He clapped his hands together.

"Fucking hell." Dean's deep voice filled the room as he ran a hand down his face, seemingly annoyed with the whole conversation.

"Yeah, fucking hell is right," I said, shaking my head.

CHAPTER 11

EVERETT

A part of me screamed not to say anything yet until we got all the facts, but the way she looked at me with her hypnotic blue eyes always had me at her mercy. We haven't got all the details just yet, but the tech gurus at the Shadows headquarters had found some interesting information out about our girl and the Irish mob. She was going to find out sooner rather than later, and when she asked me why we are protecting her, it seemed like the most opportune time to spill the beans.

Sitting beside her now at the island, eating the waffles Colson whipped up for everyone, I could sense her frustration with me. I wasn't going to let her be put in harm's way anymore. Fuck, if I hadn't already done so twice; I wasn't a fool to let it happen again. Plus, the sight of both her and Dean in so much pain was enough that I wasn't taking anymore chances with her. If I had to lock her in our safe room in the basement to ensure she was safe, then so be it. I would take that chance of her being mad at me just so she survived.

"I'm going for a swim," she announced to the room after finishing her coffee and half her waffles. It was March. The air was still chilly, but the pool was heated and that didn't stop our little fish from doing the only activity she truly loved doing, swimming.

She left the kitchen without glancing back and made her way up the stairs to her room. I continued with my waffles as did the guys, and we sat there in silence until we all finished. Placing my plate in the dishwasher, I reached for the coffeepot to pour myself another cup. I could tell I needed more caffeine to handle today.

"Pour me some, would ya, mate?" Dean said from behind me. "Better yet, we may need to make another pot."

It didn't take long for Sloan to make her way down the stairs in a red two-piece bikini, looking like a fucking snack that I so badly wanted to sink my teeth into. She didn't say anything as she made her way past us and to the sliding glass doors leading her to the pool.

"Well, I've had my share of coffee for the morning. I think a dip in the pool sounds like the perfect way to start my day. See ya, mates."

Colson's smug ass followed our girl out to the pool, leaving Dean and me alone in the kitchen.

"We can't let her get hurt again," Dean said between sipping his coffee. He was looking at her through the window as she laid her towel across one of the chairs outside and sat down at the edge of the pool.

"I don't intend on letting her get hurt again, or either of us for that matter." My tone was stern.

We stood there in the kitchen, watching Sloan kick her legs back and forth against the water as Colson joined her beside the pool. Colson was a smooth talker, and as much as I wanted to be the one sitting beside her, he was the best choice for diffusing her temper right now.

"I spoke with the guys outside this morning; they've not had any trouble so far." Dean turned to me as he spoke. Informing me about the half dozen other Shadow employees that had been tasked with watching our house for the time being.

"Good, let it fucking stay that way. I swear to the devil, whoever is behind this is going to wish they were never put on this earth." My voice was hard, and Dean continued to watch me as I watched our girl finally submerge herself in the water.

Dean placed his hand on my shoulder, aware at my anger getting ready to boil over before saying, "We'll find them, brother; I have no doubt." He made his way over to the couch with a fresh cup of coffee in hand and sat down to watch our little fish slowly start swimming laps in the pool.

Colson stayed outside with her, watching as she swam, no doubt hoping to get a round two with her in the pool. I made my way to the office, pulling my phone from my pocket and sending out a text to one of our tech guys asking if he had found anything further.

Everett: What else have you got with Wallace?

His response was quick but not with the info I was hoping for.

Tech #1: No new intel, will update when found.

Everett: Hurry up

I didn't get a response to my last message, but I wasn't expecting one. My temper was getting the best of me, and showed through my behavior. First, with Sloan in the kitchen and now with the techs. I was getting impatient; we needed to find the fuckers behind all this. The longer we waited, the more we were at risk of another attack or ambush, and I wasn't going to let that shit happen again. Not to my girl, not to my brothers.

I stayed in my office the better part of the morning, researching the most recent information obtained from our techs. Most of what Shem and his crew had been dealing with were arms deals, drugs, and the occasional murder. Nothing new when it came to the mob. Looking into his son, Sloan's father, I found that he had left Europe when he was seventeen and landed in the States. He had struggled with his addiction to cocaine and heroin at a very young age, but this wasn't surprising since his family dealt with drugs on a daily basis. It wasn't long before he began stealing from his father, which caused him to receive regular beatings from Shem. Sometimes he was even beaten by members of the mob rather than his own father.

Just as I was starting to get a headache from looking at my computer screen for too long, my phone beeped with a new message.

Tech #1: We have new information. Sending it over now. Check your email.

Everett: Understood.

All of our computers, servers, phones, any form of technology were encrypted due to our tech wizards in The Shadows making everything we sent completely secure and private to all other eyes. Just as I sent my message, my computer chimed, indicating I had a new email. I clicked on the email immediately eager to see what they had found. Quickly scanning through the email, I yelled for Dean to come to the office immediately. It didn't take him longer than thirty seconds to get to the office, no doubt worried by the tone I used to call him in here.

"What is it, mate?"

Looking up from the computer, I couldn't help my look of concern. "Has Sloan ever told you that she has siblings?" His eyebrows pinched together as if trying to remember if she mentioned having any.

"She's never said anything about having siblings.

I've always assumed she was an only child," Dean said, making his way to the vacant chair in front of the desk.

Scanning the email quickly again, I read aloud what I was sent by the tech. "Sloan's father, Frederick, apparently has a set of twins he left in Ireland before fleeing to the States. He briefly dated a girl when he was sixteen and got her pregnant. Whether he knows about these twins or not, it doesn't say. It does say the girl he dated, Maeve, did not survive the delivery and passed away after birthing a boy and a girl. Their whereabouts is currently unknown."

"So, Sloan has two half siblings and she doesn't even know about it?" Dean reiterated.

I nodded my head in agreement with Dean, and quickly reread the email to ensure I hadn't missed any other important information. After going through what the tech sent me, I sat back in my chair and looked over to Dean.

"You don't think one of her siblings wants her dead, do you?" Dean asked, giving me a hard look.

"I'm not sure. What would be their motive? Why kill a half-sibling?" I was even more confused now than I had been prior to receiving this information.

"That still doesn't help us with the fact that we were given the job to take her to Stone Fortress. Why involve us and take her to an auction for sex trafficking?" Dean stood as he asked the questions I had been thinking too.

"For fuck's sake, mate. This is not adding up or

making even a lick of sense." Dean was right that nothing was adding up, and this new information made things that much more confusing.

"So, what do we have? We need to know why The Shadows had us kidnap Sloan and take her to Osiris. Then we need to find out who is currently hunting her to steal her back or worse kill her, and now we have two siblings that could possibly be involved or could be irrelevant—we don't know. Oh, I almost forgot she is the granddaughter to the most powerful organized crime leader in all of Europe. Am I missing anything?" Dean said in a frustrated tone.

Nodding my head, I watched as Dean began pacing the office. "Doesn't seem suspicious at all, does it?" I said, sarcasm laced with every word.

I continued to watch Dean pace the floor. I could see he was still in pain from his wounds by the way he winced if he turned too quickly. Dean is a strong motherfucker, but even he couldn't hide the pain a bullet hole could create. He was deep in thought, when he stopped and leaned his massive frame against the bookshelf and placed his other hand on his hip. He looked down at the floor and closed his eyes for a moment.

"Why don't you take a seat, mate. You need to rest and let your body heal."

He just continued to stand against the bookshelf, and I could see the wheels in his mind working on overdrive. This is the man Dean is; he is furiously loyal to those he loves. He is the kind of man that won't stop searching, won't stop hunting, and when he finds the person behind all of this shit, he will undoubtedly end their time on this earth. That is, unless I find them first, then no amount of begging or pleading will stop the pain I will ensue on them. Mark my words.

CHAPTER 12

COLSON

Back and forth, down and back, Sloan had been swimming laps for what seemed like hours. I had come to realize that swimming was her source of therapy, her calming mechanism when she couldn't control the world around her. She would quite literally swim until her body gave out. For her, this was one thing in her life she could control, and so before her world comes crashing down, she takes herself to the pool and allows the world around her to disappear for the time being.

Sitting at the end of the pool with my legs dangling in the warm water, I watch her gliding so fluidly as she freestyles through the pool. This was her favorite stroke I figured out quickly; this was her go-to motion in the water. Watching her flip under the water once she reached the ends of the pool and reversing her direction was so methodical and so mesmerizing. I have no doubt that if she continued to swim competitively and go to college, she could have gone to the Olympics. Unfortunately, that's not the life God had in mind for her. Instead, she is here with us, hiding and trying to stay alive and away from those who hunt her. What a fucking life.

Sitting and watching her now, I wonder if she's happy being here with us? Does she wish to be back in the coffee shop—living her life as an average barista, serving the community one espresso at a time? Does she miss living in hostels and just making enough to pay for a bed and a roof over her head? Would she ever go back to that life if and when we find the fuckers who are looking for her? She can't leave; Everett and Dean won't let her. Shit, I won't let her. She has become one of us, and as fucked up as it is to keep someone against their free will, I'll be damned if I let her go.

"What is that pretty head of yours thinking?"

I hadn't noticed her when she stopped swimming, but there she was beside me. She was still in the water, resting her arms over the edge of the pool and peering up at me with her crystal-blue eyes.

Looking down at her, she ran her hands over her head, pushing the water across her golden hair and slicking the strands away from her face. She was breathing heavily from swimming nonstop for the past thirty minutes, and her mouth was slightly ajar to allow for more oxygen. Her lips, the perfect fullness, had a few droplets of water running down to her chin and then neck and across her exposed collar bone. She's never going to leave us, not if I had anything to do with it.

Without answering her, I hopped off the edge and into the pool, grabbing her face in my hands and crashing our lips together in a desperate kiss. I felt like a starving wolf who hadn't eaten in days and all that would satiate me was her. Her lips, her body, her touch—I wanted it all. I needed it.

She was everything I never knew I needed. All my life had been about was The Shadows, and they made it very clear in training that a woman was only good for fucking and discarding. Women would only become distractions for us, and we needed to stay away. Take what we need from them and move on. But with her, with Sloan, I could never get enough. I needed her on a deeper level. The sex was great; it was beyond great. It was fucking euphoric, hypnotic, and she was a drug I could never get enough of.

Fuck the Shadows. She was mine, and I would never toss her aside after having my way with her. She was mine and I was hers. She could never leave me, never leave us. We all had this weird connection with her that couldn't be explained. Sloan is perfectly molded into this insanely beautiful woman that fits the missing puzzle piece that is inside all three of us. We've been groomed and created into these super assassins, but have forever felt a void inside. Since we took Sloan and created this bond, my void has since dissipated. Knowing my brothers, they, too, have felt this completeness take hold since Sloan arrived.

Holding on tight to her face, I forced her lips apart with mine and started exploring her mouth. She let out a soft moan as she pressed her body into mine. I could kiss her all day and never tire, her sweet taste had my head in a frenzy and I needed all over her. I slowly pushed her body with mine until she was pressed against the side of the pool. Her hands slid beneath my swim trunks and gripped my ass, digging her nails into my skin just enough to leave a mark. That's right, my little shark, mark me as yours. Pulling back from her face I said, "You're never leaving us; you're never leaving me." My voice was laced with certainty.

"I'm no one's property, but what makes you think I *want* to leave?" She was smiling at me now, her little devious side shining through her eyes. I loved how she was a real-life Sour Patch Kid, sour and sweet.

I just smiled back as I pulled her back in for another searing kiss. Releasing her face, I wrapped my arms around her small frame and found the strings of her bikini and slowly pulled one, freeing her of the fabric. I lifted the top and discarded it on the concrete, hearing the audible slap as it landed. She had the best tits, so full, so perky that they fit so perfectly in my hands as if they were made for me.

"You're made for me, Sloan." I lowered my head and started to suck her nipple, licking and sucking what was mine. She let out another moan, and that was all the encouragement I needed. My dick was already hard and needed to be inside her. I needed to feel her warmth. I found the strings to her bottoms, and instead of being gentle I ripped them off, not wanting to wait any longer. Discarding her bottoms, I grabbed her ass, pulling her to me.

I stopped with just my tip touching her entrance, teasing her as she began to arch her body into me. "Say you'll never leave us," I whispered in her ear. She let out an impatient breath, annoyed that I was holding back until I got my answer.

"And if I don't?" She grinned at me, threading her fingers through my hair. She removed my hair tie, letting my long hair drape around my head and fall to my shoulders. She grabbed a handful of my hair and pulled my head to her face, our lips touching just barely. "I'm not yours, Colson. You're mine." She held on to my neck and wrapped her toned legs around my waist, lining up my cock with her entrance. "Now fuck me, please," she whispered into my ear, making me shiver.

With that plea I slowly pushed my cock into her until I was fully seeded. Her sweet cunt was so tight, so warm, so perfectly fit around me that I never wanted to pull out. Just as I was fully inside her, I brushed my lips against her ear and said, "Now, if you want more, you'll say you're mine and you'll never leave. I may be the sweet one, love, but don't underestimate me, especially when I want something as bad as I want you." I wanted to make myself very clear. "If you leave, there wouldn't be a place on this earth you could hide where I wouldn't find you."

She sucked in a sharp breath as I crushed my body harder into hers, her back pressed hard against the side of the pool, no doubt biting into her skin.

"Fine, I'm yours Colson. Please, I want you now."

I grinned a smile of victory as I pulled out and then back in hard, making her gasp. I continued pulling almost completely out but thrusting myself fully over and over.

Her moans quickly turned louder and louder as we found our rhythm in the pool. The water splashed between us while our movements became faster and faster. She was on the verge of her orgasm as her body tensed in my arms.

"I'm almost there, please don't stop," She begged as she let her head fall back, giving me a perfect view of her breasts bouncing in the water. My abs tensed as I tried fighting off my orgasm, wanting to come with my woman.

Her grip on my neck strengthened and her legs flexed. I knew she was about to come. She screamed my name just as we both crashed through our orgasms, her fingers digging into my flesh as my fingers did the same to her ass. Our bodies flush against one another while we savored our climaxes together. Her walls were tightening around my cock as my cum filled her up. My breathing was rapid. She moaned through her pleasure, the sweetest fucking sound I had ever heard.

Her muscles began to relax in my hold and so did mine, both our orgasms dissipating slowly. I rested my head on the crook of her neck as she rested her head on my shoulder. We stayed this way for a moment, my cock still buried deep inside her and our bodies still pinned to one another. I wanted to stay this way forever, never letting her go with her body forever pressed against mine. Two puzzle pieces fitting perfectly together.

"Perfection, that's what you are, Sloan, sweet perfection."

She nestled into my shoulder, squeezing my body just a little tighter.

"I'd say she is one fine piece of ass, should have been mine though, mate," Arno said, pulling me out of the paradise I was just in.

CHAPTER 13

SLOAN

Whipping my head around, I saw Arno standing beside Everett and Dean, his smug face plastered with a cheeky smile that reached his ears. I then heard the unmistakable metal sound of a gun cocking; Dean had his pistol pressed against the back of Arno's head, pushing ever so slightly and making his head tilt forward.

"She wasn't and never will be yours, so say another comment like that and I would be glad to put a hole in your head. I haven't killed anyone lately, and frankly I've got this itch you see. An itch that needs to be scratched."

What the fuck was Arno doing here? Suddenly feeling very exposed, I let go of Colson and wrapped my arms around my chest. Colson immediately grabbed my shoulders and spun me around so I was shielded by his own naked body.

"Turn the fuck around," Everett said to Arno as he made his way to the pool with my white robe and towel in hand. Arno did as he was told, scoffing as he did so. Everett then handed the robe to me and the towel to Colson, allowing us to cover up.

"Why the fuck is he here, Everett?" Colson asked as he wrapped the towel around his waist, his deep *V* still showing, making my core ache for more of him.

"He says he has some important information for us, regarding Sloan and who's hunting her."

I looked up at Everett with weary eyes, "Are you seriously going to trust him?"

His gaze was hard, his eyebrows furrowed. "We'll just see what info he has and talk about it together, all of us."

I sighed and looked at Arno, whose back was still to us. Dean's gun was now pointed directly at his forehead. Dean's facial expression said only one thing, death. Dean was right. Since his accident, he hadn't been able to take any jobs with The Shadows, thus, not allowing him to kill anyone. Did he truly like to kill random people? The way he stood there now, gun pressed to Arno's forehead and a look of pure murderous intent showing through his grey eyes, had me turned on. Who the fuck was I suddenly? Why was this so sexy to me, a man willing to kill another by simply saying the wrong thing about his girl? It was hot, possessive, and I was all for it.

"You two go get some clothes on and meet us in

the dining room, we have some things we need to discuss," Everett said to both Colson and me. The two of us just nodded, and Colson pressed his hand to my lower back, leading us back into the house. We both made our way to the staircase, him walking just a step behind me with his hand still on my lower back.

I stopped as soon as we got to the top and turned towards him, "What the hell kind of information do you think he has?"

Colson's face was unreadable. He stood there for a moment, thinking about his answer. He let out a long sigh before responding, "Knowing Arno, this is just another one of his games."

"How do you guys know him anyway?" I was genuinely curious. Arno seemed to be the disgusting predator type, a man unwilling to win over a girl on his own, so he resorts to sex trafficking to buy his next victim. He wasn't unattractive, rather he was quite the opposite. He was handsome, very handsome in fact, but something in his eyes screamed danger. A shiver rushed through my body as I thought to myself that victim could've been me. It could've been me, if not for the guys coming back for me, that is.

Colson didn't answer me.

"How do you know him?" I asked again, my tone a little more demanding.

He brushed his hand through his long, wet hair. He tilted his head back as the water dripped down his bare back. Without looking at me, he finally spoke, "I shouldn't be telling you this, but Arno is also one of us. He works with The Shadows along with Stefan and Jei."

I froze, my whole-body becoming tense. His voice, the voice I heard when coming out of Dean's hospital room. I knew I recognized it. It was Arno. What the actual fuck?

"What?" was all I could manage to say. I stared at the side of Colson's face; he was still looking away from me, not able to look me in the eye.

"Yes, love, he is a Shadow as well." Finally, he turned his beautiful face towards mine. "He was even a part of Dean's and your rescue operation. Along with Stefan and Jei. No matter how big of a bastard he is, or how much we three fucking despise him, he is loyal to The Shadows."

I could feel my mouth fall slightly ajar. Arno, the man who once tried to buy me at a sex trafficking auction, is also the man who helped rescue Dean and me from the horrors of the warehouse? Nothing made sense in this world they lived in. So many secrets with The Shadows that it was hard for me to keep up. But this? I never saw this coming.

"Come on, let's get dressed. If Arno came here to give info, it must be serious."

I followed him down the hall, clutching the opening to my robe so tight, my knuckles were white. Colson stopped at his room, opening the door. Before he stepped in, he turned his head to me. "Just because he's part of the organization doesn't mean we can always trust him. We are killers, Sloan. Every one of us." With that he stepped inside his room, leaving me in the hallway alone. I turned and made my way down the hallway until I reached my room.

We are killers, every one of us. What was he implying? Could I still trust the guys? Of course, I could, right? I mean they've risked their lives for me multiple times now. Was I thinking too deeply into his comment? I was getting paranoid now. *Stop it, Sloan. Get your shit together.*

Reaching my room, I grabbed a fresh pair of underwear and bra and quickly started dressing. My body was vibrating with anger, or fear. I wasn't quite sure which. Reaching behind my back, I fumbled with the bra latch, coming up unsuccessful.

"Son of a bitch," I said to myself as I backed up towards the massive floor-to-ceiling mirror that hung on the wall. Trying to see over my shoulder what I was doing, I caught a glimpse of Colson in the mirror as he entered my room. He was wearing dark jeans and a white button-up shirt. He was currently rolling up the sleeves over his forearm, with a smile of amusement across his face.

"Need some help, love?" He chuckled as he made his way over to me. Twirling his pointer finger in the air and gesturing me to turn around, I admitted defeat and did so. "You don't need to be nervous; he is in our house alone without any of his mates. He isn't that stupid to try anything while the three of us are here."

I sighed, relaxing my shoulders and letting out a

deep breath. He finished latching my bra, and I turned to retrieve my jeans, which I had placed on the bed along with a V-neck white shirt that showed a hint of my cleavage. I pulled my long hair out from my shirt and gave it a quick fluff since it was still wet from the pool. I then slid on my black ankle-high boots and turned to face Colson, who had been watching me intently.

"Okay, let's see what the prick wants," I said to him as I crossed my arms in front of my chest. Colson smiled and bit his bottom lip as he watched me unintentionally push my breasts up while folding my arms.

He walked up to me and bent his neck down towards my exposed chest. He slowly brushed his lips across my skin, making goosebumps rise as he did so. I tilted my neck back, giving him more access and closed my eyes to his touch. Fuck, he was good with knowing my sweet spots. Just as quickly as he started, he stopped. Grabbing my hand in his, he said,

"Let's not get too distracted." He then led the way from my room and back down the hall to the staircase.

Reaching the bottom of the staircase, I could make out the sounds of a discussion between Everett and Arno coming from the dining room.

"This is more complicated than you originally thought, mate." Arno's voice was unmistakable. His voice was so raspy, sounding as though his vocal cords were scarred.

"Well hurry the fuck up, and tell us why you're here." Dean, that was definitely Dean. He spoke through gritted teeth as if he was trying his hardest to maintain composure. I heard a deep chuckle from Arno, and the sound made my lips turn up in a snarl, Fuck, I hated that man.

"Be patient, mate, don't you want to wait to see the reaction on our leading lady's face when I tell her Everett's twin was the one who posted the kidnap job for her?"

I stopped at the entrance of the dining room, sucking in a gasp and drawing the attention of the room towards

"What did you just say?" I whispered.

CHAPTER 14

SLOAN

His twin. Everett has a twin brother? I had no idea he had a brother, and a twin at that. Come to think of it, I don't know anything really about the guys' families or past for that matter. Was Everett in on this as well? So many questions flipped through my head until a voice pulled me out of the trance I was in.

"Sloan, are you all right? Sloan?"

I snapped my head up and saw Everett standing in front of me. I couldn't respond. I didn't know how to respond. I felt his hands rest on the sides of my face, but I flinched back from his touch.

"Love, why don't you take a seat," Everett gestured his hand to a chair he had pulled out for me to sit in, but I was still frozen.

"You have a twin brother? He wanted me kidnapped and brought to that stone prison?"

Looking up to Everett, I could see the worry in his eyes as he inhaled deeply.

"Listen, my brother—"

I cut him off, "Were you in on it?" My words rang sharp in the air, demanding an answer. Everett placed his hands in his trouser pockets and pinched his eyebrows together.

"No," he said in a low voice. I could see he was trying to remain calm by the way his chest puffed out. He straightened his back. "My brother and I couldn't be more opposite if we tried. I haven't seen or heard from my brother in over three years, Sloan. Now if you would please take a seat, I'm sure we all would like to hear what Arno so kindly came here to tell us." Everett's tone was demanding but calm as he again gestured to the vacant chair.

I made my way to the large rectangular oak table. Sitting down, Everett pushed me towards the table, putting his face right next to my ear as he whispered, "Do you not trust me?" His hot breath made me shiver, his sandalwood-and-pine cologne invading my nostrils. I inhaled him but didn't respond.

Everett pulled out the chair beside me and sat down as Colson did the same on my opposite side. Arno then sat directly in front of me. Dean remained standing directly behind Arno, gun still drawn. Just in case. I looked over Arno's head right at Dean, my expression somber as he winked at me. I inhaled a small breath before turning my attention back to Arno. He was leaning back in his chair, arms draped over the armrests. He was wearing a black button-up shirt that was unbuttoned a little too much, exposing his chest hair. A silver cross pendant hung from a chain around his neck, making me laugh inside. No fucking way God would allow this poor excuse of a man to heaven.

"You like what you see, firecracker?"

I didn't have time to respond. Colson had already pulled out his pistol and slammed it on the table before saying, "Get to the fucking point as to why you're here."

Arno didn't look fazed that he now had two pistols pointed at him, rather he looked even more amused. He just laughed his sadistic laugh. "Calm down, boys, I'm just being friendly. No need to lose your heads."

"Like he said, mate, get to the fucking point. How the fuck do you know my brother put in the job on Sloan?" Everett said to my right, leaning back in his chair and spreading his legs wide so his left leg was now touching mine. I couldn't help but look down at the touch, my leg now becoming hot where his leg rested. He was making it hard to focus, and I really needed to focus right now.

"You forget. I, too, am a part of the organization, allowing me the technology and resources I need to find out interesting information."

He was playing with us now. His smug face saying he enjoyed every bit of knowing useful information we didn't know ourselves.

"And being part of the organization, I'm sure you are aware that all jobs created and pushed through are done so by the board members. The board in which we as employees are not authorized to know their identity. So, with that being said, mate, how did you find out a non-member of the board, better yet a non-member of the organization, created the job on Sloan?" Everett said, standing up and pushing back his chair so hard, it made a squeaking noise as it dragged along the hardwood floor.

I was suddenly extremely aware of Everett, his body giving off so much heat, he was his own furnace. His body was tense and seemed as though every muscle was flexed from trying so hard to control his temper. He then made his way behind me and placed his hands on the back of my chair.

"I'm actually feeling quite parched, Dean, would you mind fetching me a refresh—" Before Arno could finish speaking, Everett yelled over the top of me, making me jump.

"Answer the fucking question, Arno!"

My chair was now vibrating, Everett's temper rising rapidly. Fuck, this was the Everett I admit I am slightly scared of. Just answer the question, you dipshit. Arno's expression fell from his sly smirk to a deep scowl, annoyed at Everett's outburst, no doubt.

"You listen to me. There's nothing gained by me telling you anything. So, I suggest you cool your temper, my friend, and speak to me in a more respectful manner." Arno placed his elbows on the table, leaning in as he spoke. We needed this information and Everett knew that. The room was quiet as Arno and Everett stared each other down in a pissing match.

"For fuck's sake, this is such bullshit. He's lying and knows nothing; he's getting off on playing games." I pushed up from my chair, standing and turning towards the entrance to the dining room. I was done with this cockfight and couldn't stand the tension building between all four men.

I'd just reached the entrance when Arno spoke, "Just like a little princess storming off. I guess Everett's brother working for your grandfather, Granddad Wallace, wouldn't even remotely interest you?"

Fuck it all to hell. I thought to myself.

I stopped not turning around right away to face him. My shoulders rose and fell with each deep breath I was taking.

"How do you know that?" Dean's voice was not who I was expecting to speak first. I turned and looked at Everett first. His face—God, his beautiful face—was scrunched up so tight with fury, I just wanted to press my thumbs across his forehead to relax the muscles. I kept my eyes on Everett as Arno spoke again.

"I have resources, one being a mate that started working with her family, The Wallaces, a few years ago." It sounded strange hearing my last name along with the word family. I never felt as though I had a family. Certainly not my mother and father, so to hear Arno refer to the Irish mob as my family was, well, exciting.

"So, this mate of yours told you that my brother is working for the mob and that my brother is also the one to put the job up on Sloan?" Everett sounded unsure, reiterating what Arno had just said.

"You could say that. He told me they took on a new man for more security who is a little strange, to say the least. He's constantly talking about his previous hits he eliminated and all the creative ways he's killed his targets," Arno was silent for a moment before continuing. "Look, no bullshit. My mate informed me that Shem has been looking for her." He gestured to me with his hand. "He's been looking for her due to his health going all to shit. You understand, he's been looking for her in hopes she will take his position as the head of the mob. He wants you to take over the family business, firecracker." Arno clicked his tongue at me as he said firecracker.

My grandfather wants me to step into his spot as the head of the Irish fucking mob? I've never met this man before. Why in the hell does he feel like I am the best candidate for this position?

"What the hell would he want me to be in charge of his mob for? He's never met me in my life?" I directed my question right at Arno. I needed to know.

"They say, Shem is big on family and will only relinquish his power to his heir," Arno said. *Big on family, huh, just like he's big on helping his own son not turn into an abusive, cracked out, worthless excuse of a father.* I leaned my body against the arched opening of the dining room and crossed my arms over my chest.

"Let me get this right, your friend told you that Shem is looking for Sloan to have her take over the family business before he croaks? Now, how does that tell you that Cal was the one to put the job in on Sloan?" Colson had said exactly what I was thinking. Pretty sure we were all thinking that really.

"Cal had let slip his 'previous employer'"—Arno made air quotations in the air—"could find his grand-daughter."

Previous employer? What did he mean by that? I looked between the guys, all three now looking right at me. "What?" I said to the three of them. "And what do you mean about 'previous employer'?" Arno didn't answer, instead he smiled his devilishly handsome smile that I wanted to slap right off his face. He stood from his chair, brushing off his pant legs before rubbing both his hands together. I hated when men did this. They looked like a fucking house fly rubbing their hands together for no reason.

"Oh, firecracker, that's a question these three cheeky fuckers will have to answer for you." His gaze went to Dean, Colson, and then landed on Everett as he placed his hands in his pockets.

"I'm not quite understanding why, if it was Cal, that would benefit him in any way. He wouldn't do anything for others unless there was something in it for him," Colson said as he holstered his pistol that he was still holding.

"That's the million-dollar question now, isn't it? Well, my friends it seems I've overstayed my welcome. I have other business to take care of." Arno began walking towards me. I straightened my posture, trying to make myself taller, but just as Arno reached me, Dean was there. Blocking my body with his, he narrowed his eyes at Arno.

"You want us to believe that you came here out of the goodness of your heart to tell us information that could assist us in finding out who's hunting Sloan? I'm not buying it. What's in it for you?" Dean crossed his arms low in front of him, still holding his pistol.

He had a point. Why would this prick come to tell us valuable information? It didn't add up. Clearly, he was expecting some compensation for his intel, but what?

"Let's just say you owe me one for now." He patted Dean's chest with his hand before making his way past us both and towards the front door.

We all watched as he grabbed the handle and pulled the door open. One of the security guards the guys had positioned around the house met him at the entrance, ready to escort him off the grounds. Before stepping out of the foyer, Arno turned towards us one last time and said, "If you ever get bored of these three blokes, you can always come stay with me, fire-cracker." He winked at me before exiting the house, slamming the door behind him.

The slam of the door echoed throughout the large foyer, making my ears ring. No one spoke for what seemed like an eternity. I was still facing the front door when I felt a hand rest on my lower back. I turned to Dean and stepped into his chest, allowing his large frame to comfort me for a moment. He had holstered his pistol and his arms wrapped tightly around me.

"I hate that man," I said, knowing the other two could hear me as well.

"I fucking hate him, too, sweetheart," Dean agreed resting his head atop of mine.

Looking out the window in the dining room I noticed the sky starting to dim. The air would be getting cooler, the season slowly transitioning to spring. Closing my eyes, I imagined how peaceful it used to be lying under the stars on the roof of my parents' apartment building.

"Soooo, what now?" Colson said, breaking the silence in the room.

I lifted my head from Dean's chest and looked at Everett. He closed his eyes and inhaled a deep breath, before saying to the room,

"I guess we need to find Callum. Fuck," Everett practically growled as he said his brother's name.

CHAPTER 15

SLOAN

The next couple days went by, my head swimming with more questions than I had answers for. Everett has a brother, a twin brother at that, who could possibly be involved in this madness I'm now calling my life. I've never met his brother, what the hell would he want with me, let alone want me dead? Is Everett close with his brother? From the sound of Callum being mentioned, Everett didn't seem keen on finding him. I began to realize that I knew nothing of Everett's past, his family, siblings? I knew nothing about all three of the guys' pasts.

I haven't been able to sleep the past few days, my mind racing like a tornado that never slows. It seems as though the guys haven't been able to sleep as well, we've all been going throughout the days living off coffee and practically silent as we perform the monotony of life. Everett has been the most sleep deprived it seems. His eyes have developed dark shadows beneath his eyelids, his appearance being disheveled, and he hasn't left his office, just for food and coffee for the past two days. I imagine he is tracking down his brother, or I would assume.

Dean and Colson have been busy as well, mostly with Shadow's jobs. As soon as Dean fully recovered, he immediately went back to work. Although they've all been busy, one of them is always with me, always by my side. I know they're doing this to ensure I'm safe, but I can't help feeling like I'm being babysat. I can't say I hated having someone with me 24/7, I loved the fact that I was never alone. I always had someone to talk to, to enjoy the day with, to be touched by. I'd become utterly attached to these three men, and I was loving that they were all mine.

After a long day of swimming and working out with Dean in the gym to pass the time, he and I both showered and decided to call it a night early. Along with one of them always being with me during the day, I was also never alone at night. Dean, Colson and sometimes Everett always accompanied me in my bed. Everett had been a ghost most of the time, and I started to worry about how he was handling the news of his brother.

Laying across Dean's chest I waited for him to slowly slip into a deep sleep. His breathing started to slow and fall into a rhythm. Once I was sure he was asleep, I slipped out from underneath his arm and carefully crept out of bed, making sure I was not jostling the bed. Making my way to my door, I slowly turned and slipped my body through the small opening so no light from the hallway would illuminate my room. I was able to close the door without making a sound and started tiptoeing my way down the hall to Everett's room.

His bedroom door was open but no light filtered through to the hall. Reaching the door, I peaked in and noticed his bed was still made. He must not have made it to bed just yet. I decided to check the office, since this was where he spent most of his days now. Descending the stairs, I was thankful that each step was illuminated by its own light, since the whole downstairs seemed to be in the dark. Reaching the landing, I turned towards the office and was able to see a small hint of light coming from the room.

I reached the door but didn't show myself just yet. I waited, leaning against the wall to see if I could hear anything. It was utterly silent. If he was in there, he must just be sitting in his chair, because I couldn't even hear the faint clicking of his computer keyboard. Was he asleep? I was just about to poke my head around the corner when he spoke.

"Are you spying on me, baby girl?" His voice was low and playful. Smiling to myself, I stepped into the office and saw Everett sitting in his chair with his back to the door. I stood in the doorway as Everett slowly spun his chair around to face me. He was clutching a whiskey glass, holding it to his temple. He was wearing a white, long sleeve button-up that was opened completely, his abs on full display. He was in his usual black trousers, legs parted wide and one elbow resting on the arm chair while the other held his glass. My eyes gave him a once over. I hadn't noticed I was biting my lip until he spoke again.

"You see something you like?" The corner of his mouth lifted into a smirk. Entering the room, I made my way over to his desk and hopped on the table, sitting right in front of him. The polished wood was cold, and I clenched my thighs together as goose-bumps prickled over my skin. I crossed my legs and placed both my hands on the desk, leaning forward.

"I'm worried about you; I've hardly seen you these past couple days. I'm starting to get jealous of this office, since you seem to be inside it more and more." I lifted one of my eyebrows at him, hoping he got my joke. He just stared at me for a long moment, still giving me his sexy-as-fuck smirk. Finally, removing his whiskey glass from his temple, he placed it beside me on the desk. Without responding he grabbed my legs, uncrossing them and pulled himself between them, his chair's arms smacking the desk hard, the noise echoing through the room.

He then stood up, his large frame towering over me as I tilted my head up to meet his face. His body was so warm, always warm as he pressed his groin into me and threaded his fingers through my hair. My stomach ignited and filled with heat as his chest pressed against the thin tank top I was wearing. My nipples instantly hardened at his touch and just being close to this man caused a small moan to escape from my throat. Still, he didn't speak. He brushed his thumb across my cheek and then down across my lips, parting them as he brushed the smooth skin.

Closing my eyes to his touch, he continued across my jawline and down my neck, his breath heating my neck with every exhale he took. My groin throbbed as he started rocking his hips into mine, the wetness between my legs growing. I placed both my hands on his abdomen, and started running my fingers down his prominent ab muscles before grabbing his belt and pulling him into me harder.

"What have you done to me, Sloan?" His voice was a whisper as we both started panting from the tension growing between us. He grabbed my chin, and I opened my eyes to his face a mere centimeter from mine. His dark eyes pierced me like a blade. "I've never felt so protective over someone else like this. So protective that I'm willing to do whatever is necessary to keep you safe, even if that means killing my own blood."

His lips crashed to mine, taking my breath away. His kiss was savage as if he hadn't eaten for days and I was the only thing giving him life. I grabbed his collar with both hands, yanking his button-up down his shoulders. He let me go for just a second to allow his hands to thread through his sleeves and dropped his top to the ground. I grabbed his chest, digging my fingers into his skin just enough to feel the rumble of his moan beneath my fingertips.

His lips left mine, and I was about to protest until he grabbed on to my tank top and ripped it in two with one swift motion, freeing my breasts from the fabric. He pressed into my body again, kissing down my neck and kneading at my right breast with his hand. His other hand grabbed my pussy so hard I let out a small gasp.

"This is mine." He squeezed me a little harder as he lifted his head to look me in the face. "You are mine, and Lord help the people who are trying to take you from me."

"I'm yours," was all I could say back because, yes, I was his. I was his, I was Dean's, and I was Colson's. The four of us, always.

I reached for his belt and quickly unfastened it along with his trouser button. I yanked on his pants, freeing his already hard cock and wrapped my hands around the velvety soft skin. I started slowly pumping up and down his long shaft, rubbing in the bead of precum from his tip. His stomach clenched against my body as he rocked his hips in motion with my hands. He then grabbed my ass with his hands and lifted me from the desk pressing my entrance into his cock.

"Do as I say, okay, love?" he said, his voice breathy. I shook my head in agreement, not able to get the words out. He lowered me down until my feet hit the cold hardwood floor, and spun me around so I was facing the desk.

"Bend over on my desk and hold on to the edge." I

did as I was told, the coolness of the desk made me flinch as I lowered my torso along the desk and reached my arms above my head and grabbed onto the smooth edge. Turning my head to the side, I lowered my face to the desk.

"Stay still, and don't move." Again, I just shook my head. He grabbed the edges of my sleep shorts and pulled them down my long legs, exposing my ass to him. I heard a deep moan come from him as his hands rubbed along my ass and up my back. His large hands warmed my skin as he explored my body. Then he was gone. His hands left me, and I was tempted to turn around and see what he was doing, but I remembered he told me not to move.

Then, I felt him. His tongue lapped over my clit and I gasped. I lifted to my tiptoes as his tongue licked and flicked at my clit as his hands squeezed my thighs so tight, they would surely bruise. He continued licking and nipping at my folds, the sensation almost too much I couldn't help but squirm against him.

"Stay still, baby girl."

I tried, I really did, but when he inserted two fingers inside me, I saw stars. He played with me, two fingers inside me while his tongue circled my clit. It took no time at all. The wave of ecstasy that washed over me was so strong I couldn't help moaning as I rode out my orgasm. My cunt flexed and pulsed around his fingers as he slowly withdrew them from me. Coming down from my high, I lay still as he leaned into my ear.

"Now, hold on tight," he whispered in my ear. Before I knew it, he'd lined himself up with me and pushed, fully seeding himself into me. My body jerked with his thrust, and I couldn't help the small scream that escaped me. He pulled out and thrusted again, pushing deeper inside me, and my core started heating again, another orgasm building within.

His thrusts started getting faster and faster. Our bodies slapped together as his desk started scooting slightly against the hardwood floor. He then threaded his fingers through my hair, pulling my head off the desk and arching my back to him. My ass was on full display as his other hand wrapped around my hip holding me tight to him. He rode me hard and fast, a thin layer of sweat starting to bead across my skin as he continued thrusting deeper and deeper. His breathing picked up. I could tell he was close, his hand gripping my hip so hard and his other hand pulling at my hair, causing just the right amount of pain.

He let out a breathy moan as he was about to reach his climax, and thrusted two more times into me. Finding his release, he let my hair go and reached around me and found my clit once again. I was already cresting on my second orgasm and just his touch alone had me coming again. He lowered his body onto mine, his cock still deep inside me as I felt him twitch and flex while he slowly came down from his orgasm.

He started kissing the back of my neck and then down my back as his hands rubbed along the side of my body. As he reached the arch of my back, he picked me up and spun me around to face him. He sat down in his chair and pulled me onto him. Straddling him in his chair, he wrapped his arms around me and pulled my body into his as he rested his head against my chest.

We stayed like that for a long moment, holding me as he rested his head. I laid the side of my face atop his head and ran my fingers through his hair. My hands brushed across the shaved side part of his head, and then my fingers started to thread though his longer strands on top. I could stay this way forever, his strong arms wrapped around me and our bodies completely flush against one another. In this moment nothing mattered, it was just me and him, our bodies a puzzle piece matched and fitted together as one. Both of us were sweating, his release slowly dripping out of me. We were both unfazed. This was paradise—dirty, filthy, paradise.

I must've fallen asleep at some point because when I woke up, I was wrapped in a blanket, lying across the small couch in Everett's office. I was alone. The dimly lit desk lamp was still illuminating just enough to be able to see.

Looking out the window, I saw it was still pitch-black outside. I wonder what time it was. Sitting up, I rubbed my eyes and noticed I was still naked. I wrapped the blanket back around me and stood from the couch. I was about to leave the office and go find Everett, but I heard the familiar sound of an email notification on Everett's computer. Turning around, I looked at his computer and hesitated a moment before making my way back around the desk. I knew I shouldn't be snooping, but curiosity got the best of me.

I sat down in Everett's leather chair and scooted in towards the desk. I moved the computer mouse to wake the screen up and saw an email pop up across the screen. The email was unopened and I couldn't read the contents, just the subject matter.

To: King, Everett

Subject: Info on Sloan's siblings

I froze. Siblings? I have siblings? I didn't hear him; I hadn't noticed he came back in the room until he was standing behind the computer, looking down at me. I startled when I realized I was no longer alone, jumping and gasping at the sudden shock.

"Shit, I didn't mean to startle you, love." I just looked up at him, confusion etched across my face.

"What is it?" he asked me, his eyebrows pinched together with concern.

I leaned back in the chair, clutching the blanket around my body.

"I have siblings?" He closed his eyes and rubbed his hand down his face. With that reaction it must be true. I had siblings.

CHAPTER 16

EVERETT

Fuck. Standing in front of Sloan, she looked up at me with her hypnotic blue eyes. Her expression looked stunned, as she just found out she has siblings she never knew existed. Wiping down my face with my hand, I let out a sigh before answering her.

"We need to talk about this, but I want Dean and Colson here as well," I admit to her. This is something we all knew, except Sloan and I had promised my brothers that we would discuss important matters together—as a family.

She stares at me for a long while, her mouth slightly ajar as realization floods over her face.

"I have siblings," she says again, not as a question but more so as a reassurance to herself. I walk over to the chair she is sitting in and kneel down beside her. She doesn't look at me right away, she stares at the computer screen almost in a trance.

"Look at me, Sloan," I said to her in a gentle tone. She blinks a few times before she turns her head, looking down at me. "Come, let's get dressed, and I will get the guys."

Knowing there is no way she will be able to sleep after finding out she has family, let alone siblings she never knew about, I decide now is better than any to fill her in on the information our tech guys found at The Shadows.

Holding her hand, I lift her from the chair and lead her upstairs to dress and grab the guys. She's still clutching the blanket around her body as we ascend the stairs. We are both quiet, the house silent except for the sounds of our footsteps. Reaching the top of the stairs, I feel her pull my arm. Turning around, I see that she's stopped walking and is looking at the ground.

"Have you known this whole time?" she asks so quietly I can barely hear her. She lifts her head, her eyes sharp and demanding. I step towards her, resting my hands on her shoulders. She cranes her neck to look at my face as I look down at her.

"We just found out a few days ago, one of our tech guys has been looking into your past. We're trying to see if maybe someone in your past could be responsible for trying to kidnap you. Now, let's get dressed and get the guys. We can talk about this together. She didn't argue. We continued down the hall and headed to her room.

Entering her room, I notice Dean sitting on the

edge of the bed rubbing his head with his hands. With the sound of the door opening, he turns his head and gives us a look of confusion.

"I was wondering where you snuck off to, sweetheart," he says through a yawn. Standing up, he makes his way over to us but stops when he sees Sloan's face.

"What's wrong, what's happened?" he asks, his voice dark. He closed the gap between him and Sloan in two long strides, grabbing on to her shoulder and tilting her face up to his. "What's going on, are you hurt?" He examined her, realizing she was naked underneath the blanket she was gripping around her. When she didn't answer him, he turned to me, with rage bubbling in his chest.

"What the fuck is going on, Everett?" I rested my hand on his shoulder before answering him,

"It's okay, Dean, she's fine," I said, walking over to her dresser to get her some clothes.

"Fine, that's it? I'm just fine?" Anger coated every word she spoke. "I just found out I have siblings and all you can say is I'm fine?" Dean and I both looked at each other, realization setting in as his brows furrowed.

"Please, love, let's just get dressed and talk about this when we are all together." She was about to respond but was interrupted.

"What's going on in here, huh?" Colson said from behind Sloan, scaring her by his sudden presence and making her jump. "Oh shit, sorry, I didn't mean to scare you." He placed his hand on Sloan's neck, tilting her head to him and placing a kiss on her forehead. Colson was wearing all black, his pistols placed in his shoulder holsters he had hanging loosely over his shoulders. He'd been tasked with more and more jobs recently, his unique set of stealth and skills needed to eliminate specific targets.

He yawned as he looked between Dean and me. I grabbed shorts and a T-shirt for Sloan, along with a pair of panties from her dresser and laid them on the bed.

"Sloan, get dressed and meet us in the living room."

I could tell she wanted to say something but decided against it, grabbing her clothes and heading for her bathroom. I nodded my head to the guys and made my way to the door on my way to the living room. I heard Colson behind me say, "What the hell have I missed, mate?"

He must have addressed the question to Dean because he answered, "Your guess is as good as mine. Let's go."

"Fuck, let me change first, I'll meet you down there." I then heard hurried footsteps as Colson headed to his room to change. Dean started behind me, reaching the top of the stairs as I reached the bottom.

It didn't take long for Colson to get to the living room, hell, he was practically dressing himself as he entered the room, pulling on his white T-shirt as he found a spot on the couch. I noticed a faint bruise starting on the left side of his rib cage before he pulled the shirt fully on.

"Rough night?" I asked him as he sighed and practically fell back onto the couch.

"A little mishap, but nothing I couldn't handle. Thanks for the concern, though, mate." He winked and blew a kiss at me. Fucker. Colson sat next to Dean, who was sitting to his right leaning on the arm of the couch, his legs spread wide and taking up a large portion of the couch. Colson started pulling his long sandy-blond hair into a bun, when I heard Sloan's footsteps enter the living room.

She was in black lounge sweats, and a navy-blue long sleeve shirt. Not the clothes I had set out for her. She made her way over to the sofa and sat beside me before curling her legs into her chest and wrapping her arms around them.

"So, tell me, how many siblings do I have?"

Colson immediately snapped his head up as he fastened his man bun, looking right at Sloan. "Oh shit, who told her?" He turned his head, raising an eyebrow at me.

"Please don't talk as if I'm not sitting right here. How many?" she asked again, turning and looking at me. I grabbed a water bottle from the fridge before sitting down and took a sip before answering her.

"Right now, we know for sure you have two half siblings. Twins, actually. Your father had gotten a woman pregnant in Ireland before leaving her and traveling to the States. From what we could gather, they're around three years older than you. A male and a female." I paused, giving her a moment to absorb the information.

"What are their names?"

"Not sure yet; we found out a few days ago." I took another swig of my water, waiting for her to speak again.

"Do you know where they are now? Can I meet them?" She sounded hopeful, almost happy at the thought of having siblings.

"We don't. All we know is they're somewhere in Ireland, and that their mother passed away while giving birth." I watched her as her head fell low.

"How awful." If there was one thing I've learned about Sloan, it's that she has a heart of gold. After Dean told me all the details of the warehouse and how she practically shielded his body with hers, I realized she would do just about anything for the ones she cared for. The room was silent for a moment; Dean, Colson, and I allowed time for Sloan to process what she'd just learned. I was about to ask if she had any more questions, when she finally spoke.

"When you find out where they are exactly, I want to meet them."

I dreaded having to tell her the answer to that statement. We planned on one day Sloan being able to meet her siblings; however, we would be meeting the twins first to ensure their intentions were good. Plus, we still didn't know who was out to get her.

"Listen, doll, we want you to meet them, we really do. However, we aren't sure if they're good company yet. Once they're found, we plan on setting up a meeting with them, but just us three. We need to make sure you're safe."

I was thankful Dean spoke up, allowing the heat of keeping this secret from her to be equally dispersed between the three of us. Sloan jumped from where she was sitting on the couch and said, "What, are you kidding me? No, I'm coming with you guys; they're my siblings!"

To be honest, I would have been shocked if she didn't react like this. I understood where she was coming from, but to be fair, we knew nothing about these two and her safety is our top priority. I reached for her hand to pull her back to the couch, but she pulled away from me.

"Sit down, Sloan." My tone was stern, and I was not in the mood to lose my temper tonight. She stood her ground. "Sit down, now." My voice, a low growl.

She gave me a hard look and crossed her arms across her chest before saying, "I've never felt as though I had a family, not once in my life. Now you're telling me that I have siblings and refusing me to meet them?" She pouted with her full lips curled into a frown. I stood up because I hated when people looked down at me.

"We aren't saying you won't ever meet them. We are saying your safety is our priority, so we need to make sure they have no plans of killing you." Her eyebrows relaxed, and she started to understand how much she truly meant to the three of us. "I'm not willing to risk putting you in danger, and I'm pretty sure Dean and Colson feel the same."

She turned around, looking at the guys as they both nodded in agreement. I could see she was starting to understand, and the anger began relaxing off her shoulders.

"Fine, when will you know their location?" she asked us, sounding defeated, her head lowered to the floor.

"Our tech guys are working on it as we speak." I brushed a strand of her hair behind her ear and tilted her neck up, forcing her to look at me. "Now since that is out of the way, let's say we all go to bed." I was exhausted because I hadn't been in bed at all yet, nor had Colson.

"Amen to that, mate," Colson said through a yawn. "What do you say, sweetheart, need a cuddle buddy?" Colson winked at Sloan, but before she could answer Dean had swung his arms around her waist and hoisted her over his shoulder.

"Not a chance. She was sleeping with me until this whole mess came up. She's finishing the night with me. Night, gents." Dean slapped Sloan's ass as he made his way to the stairs. She was giggling as her hair hung in her face, but she lifted her head up, pushing against Dean's back to blow both of us a kiss goodnight.

"Sloan, I call dibs tomorrow night!" Colson yelled

as we watched her hair swing around the corner and out of sight.

"Fucker," Colson mumbled, making me laugh. I clapped him on the back, then I headed for bed, thoroughly exhausted. I'd start searching harder for the twins tomorrow, but for now I needed rest.

CHAPTER 17

SLOAN

Sitting at the kitchen island, I sipped my coffee and still couldn't wrap my head around the fact that I had siblings. It'd been two days now since I found out and the shock of this was still fresh in my head. How could I have gone my whole life never knowing this? We shared the same father, but that meant nothing since he was never there to raise them. Their mother died, so who raised them? Do they know our grandfather is essentially a mob boss?

I closed my eyes to the pain that was now throbbing in my head from it racing so much. I inhaled a deep breath before letting it out and taking another sip of coffee.

"If you keep it up like that, you're going to get wrinkles in that pretty little forehead of yours," Dean said from where he sat beside me. He, too, was drinking his coffee, but also working on his laptop at the island.

I sighed and smirked at him as he continued looking at his screen. Staring at the side of his face, I couldn't help admiring how incredibly handsome he was. His strong, sharp jaw flexed as he clenched his teeth together over and over again. I noticed he did this a lot when he was working; it was a twitch for him. Where some people tapped their feet while concentrating, Dean clenched his jaw. It was subtle, but I noticed, especially on mornings like these. Mornings where it was just the two of us drinking our coffee in silence and just allowing our bodies to wake up slowly.

"What are you working on?" I asked, turning back to where my plate of fruit lay on the island.

"If I told you, I'd have to kill you." I knew he was joking, but a part of me thought this statement would've been real if anyone else other than me would have asked him. I wasn't even supposed to know The Shadows existed, let alone their inner workings.

"Where's Colson?" I looked around, seeing if I had missed him sleeping on the couch or if he truly wasn't here. I hadn't seen him last night or this morning.

"Curious little bee today, aren't we?" I glanced over, Dean now looking at me with one of his eyebrows raised and a half smile that made my core heat. I scoffed and tilted my head at him. "He'll be back this evening. He's been, uhm, working," he debated the words to use.

"You can say it. I already know he's 'killing' people." I used my fingers as air quotes emphasizing my words. He chuckled at my comment.

"Cute, very cute." he said, turning back to his computer.

Colson had been on a lot of jobs recently, more than Dean and Everett as a matter of fact. I was genuinely curious; how did they choose the jobs for each person to fulfill? I didn't bother asking this question, since I already knew I wouldn't get an answer from Dean.

Finishing my coffee, I stood up and rinsed my dishes in the sink and placed them in the dishwasher. Closing the door, I placed my hands on the counter before asking, "So, what's on the agenda for today?" Dean lifted his eyes from over his computer, giving me a curious look. I lifted an eyebrow at him, waiting for a response. He then closed his laptop and gave me a mischievous look.

"You and I are going to work on self-defense techniques." Well, I wasn't expecting that, but he had my full attention.

"Self-defense?"

"Yes, baby girl. Self-defense." He stood from his stool and made his way over to me from around the island. He grabbed my hips with his hands and turned my body, so my back was now up against the cabinets. Raising his hands, he placed one on each side of my face, flat against the cabinets. His chest brushed against mine, causing my nipples to harden. He leaned his face down to mine, lips millimeters apart.

"You need to know how to defend yourself. Like right now." He leaned his body into mine, making it hard for me to squirm beneath him. "How would you get out of this scenario?"

I lifted my hands and pressed them against his chest, but he was too heavy. I pressed harder as he was pressing into me. I couldn't move him; it was like I was pushing a brick wall. He had me completely blocked with his body. The sad part was, he was smiling down at me, like it was too easy to incapacitate me.

I stopped pushing and let my arms fall by my side.

"Fine, you win. I suppose it wouldn't hurt to know how to protect myself better," I admitted, slightly ashamed of my lack of strength.

"Atta girl." He leaned down and kissed my forehead, making my knees weak.

"Come with me." Grabbing my hand, he led me out of the kitchen and down the long hallway past the garage and through the gym doors. I'd been in the gym numerous times, running on the treadmill and doing some weight training to keep me in shape, but when Dean led me to the corner of the gym that was laid out like a wrestling arena, I started to get butterflies in my stomach. I was scrappy and knew a few tricks to take down an opponent, a skill I taught myself after numerous incidents as a child and being around my parents' friends. I had taught myself to survive.

He pulled me to the mat and positioned himself in front of me.

"Show me what you know about protecting yourself." He let my hand go and stepped back a foot outstretching his arms to allow full access to his body for demonstration.

"Are you serious?" I cocked my head at him, not really sure if he was serious or not. He lowered his arms and gave me a comforting smile.

"Show me anything you know about fighting off an attacker. I want to see what you already know. Pretend I'm an attacker, and you need to get away." He patted his chest with both hands, encouraging me to fight him.

I bent my knees slightly and got into what I felt was a good offensive position and waited for him to strike. Walking up to me, he reached out his hand to me, but I swatted it away before he could touch me.

"Good," he said and then started to sidestep around me. I kept my front to him, not allowing him to get behind me. We circled one another as I waited for him to strike again. He reached his arm out again, but this time as I tried to swat him away, he spun to the opposite side, getting behind me and wrapping his arms tightly around my upper body.

"See what I did there? You were so focused on my

hand, you didn't anticipate my next move." I grunted and tried to free myself from his hold, but he was too strong.

"Men are strong, Sloan. You need to be able to anticipate our moves before acting; that way no one has the chance to get their hands on you. This will be your best chance at escaping." He let me go and circled me once more as he spoke. I straightened my back and suddenly became very aware of him stalking around me.

Keeping my head up, I lowered my eyes to watch his steps. He continued walking around me and I stayed utterly still, cementing myself to the mat. Just then I noticed one of his legs step back behind him and then jerk as he lunged forward at me from the side. I quickly spun away from him just as he was about to wrap his arms around me once more. He grabbed at the air as he turned to see I had already maneuvered away from his strike.

"Just like that, baby girl, just like that." He narrowed his eyes on me and smiled at how quickly I was able to dart away. I smiled back at him, shocked that I was able to move that quickly. Dropping my head to catch my breath, I was suddenly taken to the ground. Lifted from the mat and tackled flat on my back. He was on top of me, his huge frame towering over me. "Never, I mean never, let your guard down."

I was panting heavily as he straddled my hips and pinned my arms above my head. As quick as I thought I had moved, he was quicker, so much quicker. We stared at each other a moment, catching our breaths, when I started feeling the familiar throb of my core as he pressed himself into me.

He lowered his head to my neck and started kissing ever so softly up and down and around the back of my ear, sending a shiver throughout my body. I arched my back to him, pressing my now throbbing pussy into the familiar bulge that was not well hidden beneath his sweatpants. All of a sudden, I was blistering hot. My skin felt like a furnace from deep in my core that spread throughout my body. A bead of sweat made its way down my chest and between my breasts.

Since the incident at the warehouse, Dean and I had not been intimate with one another. I allowed his body to fully heal, not wanting to further injure his already wounded body. It was torture, not being able to touch him how I wanted, and I knew he felt the same. On numerous occasions, I had to turn him down—it being too soon for sex. But at this moment, he was fully healed. No more stitches, no more bandages, no way of reinjuring or tearing open his wounds. Frankly, it was a miracle the both of us had made it this long without fucking each other wild.

His lips trailed down the side of my neck, sucking at the sensitive spot behind my ear. His grip on my wrist got a little tighter as he grinded himself into my eager pussy.

"I've waited too long for this, baby. You're mine now." I moaned my approval as his lips met mine, and we started devouring each other's mouths. Hunger for the pleasure and feel of him inside me had me acting primal. I tore my wrists from his grasp and viciously tore at his shirt, yanking him free. His chest gleamed with a thin layer of sweat coating his perfectly imperfect skin. Now covered in cigar scars and a gunshot wound, I couldn't help my fingers as they trailed along every imperfection, down his muscular chest.

"Do they still hurt?" I couldn't help the question, mainly because of my own scars. Some days they felt as though they were still on fire, the sizzle of skin bubbling underneath the fresh skin that grew in wrinkled and discolored.

"Do yours?" he asked me, since we now both shared more matching burn marks. I didn't answer him, because him answering my question with a question was all the understanding I needed.

He grabbed the hem of my tank top and tore the fabric down the middle exposing my bra and bare abdomen. He didn't hesitate. He reached around my back and unfasted my bar with one hand, making me smirk at his skills with unhooking a bra, and tossed it across the gym.

"You're kind of a master at that," I joked with him, but he only gave me a crooked smile before claiming my mouth once again. His chest pressed against my bare breasts, rubbing my nipples into a hard point. I wrapped my arms around his neck, holding his mouth to mine as I bit his bottom lip, pulling at it slowly. A deep groan came from his chest, the vibration rippling across my chest.

Before I knew it, his arms wrapped around my thighs, pulling me off the mat and wrapping around Dean's waist. He moved so quickly that the sudden position forced a small squeak to slip from my mouth. He carried me across the gym and to the lounge chairs that were lined against the far wall. One long couch and two recliner style chairs sat beside each end of the couch. Dean sat us both down right in the center of the couch.

It was soft, really soft, the cushions themselves were like a memory foam texture that formed around your body as you sat. A dark gray microfiber fabric covered the cushions, adding to the softness. Dean leaned us back on the couch, my breasts now at the perfect level to his face. His mouth immediately came down on one of my breasts as he started sucking and nipping at my nipple, causing goosebumps to prickle over my skin.

Tilting my head back, I allow for him to devour me as if I'm his very own personal buffet. I lightly scratched my nails along the back of his neck and along his scalp. His hair had grown out some on top, but the sides still gave off the familiar feeling of being freshly shaved. His hands grabbed my waist, squeezing just enough to make my obliques flex against his touch, as he started pushing his cock to my aching core.

"Take these off, or I will tear them off of you too."

His tone was demanding and forceful. I did as he asked, quickly stepping off his lap and pulling my shorts and panties down and around my ankles. Kicking them off, he pulled the waist of his sweats down, releasing his enormous erection—hard and ready. Just as I was about to sit back on his lap, I decided otherwise. Instead, I pulled my hair back over my shoulders and knelt down in front of him. Staring up at his steel-gray eyes, I licked my lips before taking him into my mouth.

His length was too much, I couldn't fit all of him into my mouth, even when I have no gag reflex. I wrapped my hand around the base of his length and started sucking and moving up and down at a pace that had his legs flexing against my face. He let out a deep moan and placed both his hands on my head, threading his fingers through my hair. He encouraged me to go deeper, pushing my head deeper and deeper along his length.

"Fuck, baby girl, that's it, take all of me," he spoke through gritted teeth as he let his head fall back on the couch. He started pushing me faster and faster until I thought he may come, but just as his cock twitched in my throat, he lifted me up from underneath my arms and sat me down on his lap, fully seeding himself into my pussy. I sucked in a breath of air as he slammed my body down on top of him.

"Now hold on tight." His devilish grin spread across his face as he began bucking and fucking me so hard and fast, it didn't take me long to feel the build of an orgasm coming from deep in my core. Our breathing was erratic and heavy as pleasure and pain shot between us. His hands squeezed down on my hip bones as I steadied myself on his shoulders. My tits bouncing as he fucked me harder and harder. I couldn't hold back and let out a desperate moan as my orgasm sent shock waves throughout my body, making every muscle flex as I rode out the waves of pleasure, Dean followed right behind me as he bucked one last time.

"Fuckkk," he breathed as his cock twitched and flexed inside me. He pulled my body into his, wrapping his arms around my back and resting his head atop my breasts as he delivered soft kisses. I leaned my head down, meeting him, and we stayed that way until we could catch our breaths again.

I could've stayed just like that for the rest of my life, but the sound of the gym door startled me back to reality.

"I see I've missed all the fun," Everett's voice filled the room, as a small chuckle came from Dean. "When you two get yourselves together, meet me in the living room. I have news on Callum." With that, he turned and left the gym as quickly as he came.

I lifted my head from Dean, and we both shared a look of concern. He gave me one last kiss on my chest before saying,

"Let's go love, I haven't heard or seen Cal in well over eight years. This ought to be interesting," We both stood up and dressed, making our way from the

gym, but not before I made a quick stop at the bathroom to clean myself up a bit. Cleaning up fast, I
made my way down the hallway to meet with the
guys, my heart beating so fast I could hear the
pounding in my ears.

Turning the corner to the living room, I froze when
I heard Everett tell Dean, "He knows where we live,
mate, it's not safe for Sloan here anymore."

CHAPTER 18

COLSON

My eyelids are heavy as I clenched the steering wheel so tight my knuckles began turning white. I can't shake the image of the dozens of little girls, each one sitting in fucking dog crates all lined up inside an open warehouse. All the girls were in little-to-no clothing, hugging their knees so tight, trying to keep warm. Those girls deserved so much better. The images of their watery eyes will haunt me for the rest of my life.

My recent jobs have been tasked to me specifically for my unique set of skills. I've been trained to be proficient at shooting, sniper shots to be exact. Although we are all trained in weaponry, my shots have yet to miss their targets. You could say I'm the best when it comes to long distance shots, or so I've been told. With the rise of sex trafficking all around

Europe, I've been sent on more jobs than my brothers in the past few months.

My muscles ache and there's a pounding in my head that feels like someone is whisking my brain with an automatic mixer. Fuck I'm tired. I crank the AC and turn the vent to my face to help keep me awake. You're almost there, Colson, another ten minutes and you can crawl into bed and slowly slip into the abyss.

My phone chimes, and I look down to see a text message from Everett. I don't check it right away, one being that I'm driving, two being that I just don't care right now. I yawn and thank the man above that I've reached the driveway. Turning into our estate, I stop at the keypad and type in my code. The big, black iron gates slowly swing open, and I accelerate my Jaguar down the long driveway.

I expect to see the lights out, since it's well past midnight, but I can see the dimly lit lights shining through the window in the office. Knowing it's probably Everett, because the man hasn't been sleeping since learning about his brother's involvement with Sloan, I pick up my phone and read his message.

Everett: Come to the office when you get here. Got some news.

Shit, that can't be good. I pull my car into the garage and put it in park, but don't immediately get out. I lean my head back against the seat and close my eyes. Dark brown eyes, full of tears cascading down her angelic face flashes in my mind. Girls that couldn't be older than thirteen, all taken from their families and treated like dogs—all for the pleasure of sick, psychotic fucks. My chest aches, and I bang my hands against the steering wheel.

After eliminating the targets, I made my way down from my access point. I stationed myself beside the warehouse where the girls were being held, at the highest window, giving me full view of the fucking pedophiles guarding the girls. After informing my crew that all targets had been dealt with, the clean-up crew and extraction teams hurried in to get the girls.

I usually identify the target, eliminate said targets and leave, but this job I chose to stay at my location, watching until all the girls were safe. Looking through my scope, I landed on a little girl, she looked to be the youngest. So small, so innocent, so frightened. She was in nothing but a cropped-off shirt and panties. The temperature right now was well in the forties. There was no mistaking that she was shaking from the cold. I doubted she would have made it through the night. Hypothermia would have claimed her before anything else.

Her waist-long brown hair was matted to her back and shoulders. Her skin was so filthy, so covered in dirt I couldn't distinguish between her bruises and the caked-on mud. Her eyes were like faucets, tears at a constant flow and her teeth chattering. My blood boiled at the state of this poor girl. I started to regret killing her captors so quickly. I would have much rather done them off slower, more painful, more gruesome. I wanted to make their deaths so excruciating that they would've begged me for a merciful death.

A knock at my window brought me out of my trance, and I opened my eyes to Everett standing beside my door looking tense. I unbuckled and opened my door, swinging my exhausted legs out of the car.

"You all right, mate?" Everett asked, genuinely looking concerned as I rubbed my eyes.

"Never better," I lied. Honestly, I've never wanted my brothers, or anyone else within our corporation, to know that some jobs, like the one I was just on, fucked with my head, royally. This is our job. I'm not the only one who's seen some shit, so why should I burden them with my sobs, when I know damn well they've had to deal with chaos too?

Everett patted me on the back, and we both walked into the house, silence filling the foyer and only the speckle of light coming for the office. I made my way in and dropped my weary body down on the couch.

"I'm all ears, mate," I said through a yawn as I watched Everett sit in his chair behind the desk. The dark rings that were now prominent below his eyes only emphasize how little sleep he was getting. Picking up his crystal glass and swirling the amber liquid around, he tipped it up to his mouth, downing the remaining contents. He cleared his throat before saying, "Callum knows this location; Sloan isn't safe here." His eyes were dark as he spoke, anger from just speaking of his brother apparent as he spat his name. Letting my hair down from the bun it was in, I shook my head and rubbed my fingers through the strands.

"How do we know this?" I asked as I continued scratching my scalp. Fuck that feels amazing.

"I had the pleasure of speaking with him personally. It was almost like he was expecting me to contact him." He shook his head, confusion etched across his face. "I don't understand, Colson, we haven't heard from him in what eight or nine years, and now he shows up out of fuck knows where and could be connected with Sloan? It doesn't make sense." He wiped his hand down his face before continuing. "I was able to find a number with the tech at the headquarters, and when I called him, the first thing that fucker says was, I've been waiting for your call, brother."

"What did he say after that?" I asked, leaning my elbows on my knees and arching my back. He shook his head again; I could see his anger building and his annoyance reaching all new levels. What Dean and I know about Callum is that he's a pretentious, arrogant prick that acts as though the world owes him something for simply being alive and gracing us all with his presence. It's night and day when it comes to Everett and Callum, the only thing they have in common is that they are identical in every way when it comes to appearance. A perfect copy and paste with two human beings. If it wasn't for the tattoos being different, I wouldn't be able to tell the difference, until they opened their mouths.

It's truly wild how both of them have tattoos in all the same places visible to the human eye, although they both have ink, they both display different art on their bodies. So, neither of them have similar designs, just the same placement. While Everett has Scandinavian symbols going up the sides of his scalp, Callum has Egyptian script along his scalp. At least the last time I saw him it was—if he's changed it within the last eight years, I'm not sure.

"Before I could even ask a single fucking question, he said, you made a mistake going back for the girl; now I have to do what I was trying to avoid and actually kill her. I'll be seeing you and your dog's soon, leave the gate open for me," Everett said, the vein in his temple becoming more visible with every word he spoke. "He hung up after that. I tried to call him back but the line was dead."

I looked down at my fingers as I anxiously fiddled and rolled my thumbs around one another. Looking up and meeting his gaze, I said, "How do you know he knows our location if that's all he said?"

"You and I both know Cal is not someone to say some shit like, leave the gate open for me, if he didn't want us to know he's aware of our home. He's a cryptic fuck who loves to keep your mind going in hopes we fuck up and don't read between his lines."

Everett was right, Cal is the type that gets off on playing games. From his quick chat with his brother, it sounds like Cal is in fact intertwined with this whole mess of things involving our girl.

"Fuck, mate. What do we do then? Where do we go?" I asked, leaning back on the couch and spreading my legs wide. He, too, leaned back in his chair before he said, "We take her to the castle; that's the one location I know for a fact Callum doesn't know about." I gave him a smirk; I loved the castle and he knew it. He returned the smirk, and I slapped my thighs with my hands.

"To the fucking castle then, right." Out of all the properties we owned, the castle, or what we referred to it as, is without a doubt the most tranquil and somber place we own. If it were up to me, we would live their full time. The only downfall is the location being quite a distance from the headquarters. This makes it a bitch getting to and from jobs. Other than that, the castle is a princess's dream, and I can't wait to show Sloan.

CHAPTER 19

SLOAN

Everett had told us a couple days ago we would soon be leaving the house and traveling to another property the guys owned. I was excited for a change in scenery; however, the reason for us having to leave left me weary. Callum knows where we are. At this very moment he knows where I sleep, where I eat, and I'm no longer safe in this house. He hasn't told me where we're going exactly, just that I won't be disappointed. Whatever the hell that means. As long as I'm with my boys, I don't care where we go.

After a quick night swim, I decided to skip dinner and head straight to bed. My eyelids becoming so heavy I could barely stand in the shower without nodding off. Quickly, I washed and got out, wrapping my large fluffy robe around me. I fell to my bed and dozed off before I could even get dressed. Heavy footsteps had me jerking from my sleep when I noticed I was now tucked in my bed, my robe wrapped around me tight. One of the guys must have gotten me into bed properly, but I was alone. I rarely, if ever, slept alone since being here.

Getting out of bed, I decided I would see who was up at this hour. Wondering what time it was, I looked around the room and saw the clock on the nightstand illuminated with the number 2:30. Damn, I was sleeping hard. Making my way to the door, I slowly opened it and noticed the hall lights shining bright down the long corridor. From the sound of the footsteps, it sounded like whoever it was had made their way down the stairs.

It was at this moment I realized if I were in a horror movie, I would surely be the character to die after following the mysterious footsteps around the quiet and ominous mansion. Curiosity always kills the cat, but I was already up and had a feeling it was one of the guys anyway. Well, I hoped it was one of them.

Being light on my feet, I tiptoed down the hall and down the stairs. I saw the soft light of the kitchen and headed for the arched entrance. It was quiet, the whole house was, not a sound I could hear besides the soft padding of my bare feet on the tile floor. Peaking my head in, I saw a figure leaning on the island with a crystal tumbler in their hand. Their head was down, and a cascade of hair fell around their face.

"Colson?" I whispered, not wanting to scare him. "Are you okay?" He didn't stir right away, just stayed leaning on the island, no shirt and a pair of loose-fitting sweats hung low around his slim waist.

"Colson?" I said again, entering the kitchen and making my way over to him. He looked up this time, brushing his long hair back from his face.

"Hey, baby girl, what are you doing up so late?" His voice low, exhaustion evident by the way his voice cracked through his words.

"I could ask you the same thing." I hopped on the island beside him and adjusted my robe so my bare ass wouldn't touch the cold granite. He stood up straight and tossed back the remaining liquid in his glass, taking it all in one gulp.

Setting his glass down, he turned his back around, grabbing the decanter and filling his glass halfway before taking another sip. Dark circles heavily lined beneath his eyes, and his face was two shades of red indicating he was, in fact, intoxicated. I had never seen him this way before, and my insides ached for him.

"Are you okay?" I placed my hand on his cheek as he lowered his head once again, making it so I couldn't see his face. This wasn't Colson. His body was swaying back and forth, and his general appearance was foggy, disheveled, but above all else his face looked broken.

Hopping off the island, I spun his body around so he could lean on the island for support as I stood in front of him. I grabbed his face with both my hands and looked into his face. His eyes were filled with tears and where they were normally white, they were now red. He was very drunk.

"Colson, what's going on? Why are you drinking alone down here?" He didn't respond. His head bobbed in my hands, and I feared he would pass out any moment.

"Please, say something." Still, he remained silent. I debated calling for one of the guys to help me get him to bed, but just as I was about to, his body began sliding down the island and I couldn't hold him upright anymore. I was strong, but not holding a grown man's deadweight strong. However, I was able to slow his fall as we both made our way to the floor, my arms wrapped around his waist, squeezing him and holding as tight as I could so as not to crash to the tile.

As we slowly fell to the floor, his head leaned back against the bottom cabinets with a loud thud. Wincing at the pain that surely caused him, I tilted his head up so he wasn't slumped over.

"Colson, what is going on with you? I've never seen you—"

He cut me off. "Haven't seen me drunk before. Well, here I am," he said, lifting his arms to the side, gesturing to his drunken state. "Just a man, drunk in his own house, trying to erase the memories of those poor girls." His voice cracked as he spoke of the girls, but what girls he was referring to, I was unsure.

"What girls?" I asked him, holding his head up once again as he started to slump over once more. He closed his eyes, breathing in a deep breath.

"Nothing, forget it, love," he spoke so quietly I could hardly hear him. "I'm not paid to care; I'm paid to kill. Mission done, move on, Colson, you fucking pussy." It dawned on me, Colson had been sent on more jobs recently than Dean and Everett. I wondered if he was talking about something that happened on a job. I can't imagine the shit he's seen, what they've all seen.

I was about to ask him what he was referring to, but when I lifted his head once again, he was out cold. The alcohol and exhaustion had taken over as his head rested in my hands and the rest of him lay still on the tile floor.

Fuck, what was I going to do with him, how would I get him off to bed? I sure as hell couldn't carry him, and I didn't want to drag him either. Looking around the kitchen, for what exactly I wasn't sure, but I needed to do something. Laying Colson's head and upper body slowly to the floor, I rested his head on a tea towel that was draped over the oven handle.

Standing up, I started making my way back to the stairs to get the guys, but a huge shadow stood in front of me as I collided with their chest. The sudden appearance had me yelp with fear.

"Jesus, Everett. You scared the fuck out of me."

Looking up, Everett gave me a cheeky smile before

looking over my head to Colson, where his smile quickly faded.

"Rough night?" he asked, turning his gaze down to me.

"I don't know what's going on. I woke up and found him down here drinking." I turned to look at Colson, who was now lying on the tile floor, his torso slowly rising and falling with every breath.

"Has he said anything to you?"

"No, not directly, at least. He was saying something about the girls. Then he passed out." I walked over to him and knelt down beside his sleeping body. I brushed his hair back from his face. He looked so beaten down, so physically and emotionally drained. Lying there, he looked like a child, half clothed and curled up on his side, hair a mess, and mouth slightly ajar. The kitchen was quiet except for the rhythmic sounds of Colson's breathing.

"What do we do, Everett? I'm worried about him. Has he ever acted like this before?" I looked up at Everett, his expression unreadable. He stood in the entrance way, ramrod straight, arms at his side, and his eyes locked on to mine. He wore dark jeans and a dark, long sleeve top. Just as I was about to open my mouth, he spoke first.

"It comes with the job, Sloan. He knew what this life entailed; we all did." He sighed heavily. "Not like we would've chosen this for our lives, but no use wailing now." Everett came over beside us, kneeling down beside Colson's head.

"He was dealt a shitty hand of cards when he was young. His own father sold him to pay off a debt rather than being killed himself. Piece of shit was killed anyway after sending Colson away. Not many people can forget about that type of abandonment." Everett then scooped up Colson's neck with one arm and then his legs with his other, picking him up as if he weighed nothing.

"I'd say he'd sleep better in his own bed; wouldn't you think?" He adjusted Colson's deadweight and tilted his head to the stairs, allowing me to take the lead.

I gave Everett a sad smile before leading the way up the stairs and towards Colson's room. Stopping at the closed door, I turned the knob and pushed it open, allowing Everett to step in first. I didn't turn on the light. I just left the door fully open so Everett could use the lights from the hallway to maneuver his way to the bed. Everett placed Colson on the bed, making sure he was not on the edge, just in case he rolled.

Once he was safely in his bed, Everett nodded once towards my room.

"Let's go, love, you need to get your rest as well." I secretly loved how bossy Everett was. I turned and started down the hall, Everett's hand resting on my lower back as he followed close behind. I pushed open my room, the bathroom light illuminating the room for us. Stepping in, I stopped at my dresser and started fishing out some panties and a nightshirt but was stopped short.

"You won't be needing those tonight." Everett's tone was full of mischief. Standing at my back, he reached his arms around my waist and pulled at my robe, letting the strings fall by my side. He kissed my neck so lightly, sending a shiver throughout my body. Tilting my head to the side to give him better access, I felt his hands grab the collar of my robe and soon the soft fabric slid down my shoulders and then my arms.

"I thought you wanted me to get some rest?" I said jokingly, because the last thing I wanted to do right now was sleep. His warm breath skated across my neck and behind my ear as he whispered, "If you want to sleep, my dear, I won't stop you." I could feel his lips smiling against my skin, my body pressing against his front, my ass grinding against the bulge in his jeans. I laid my head back against the crook of his neck, as he placed one finger between my breasts and slowly dragged his hand down my abdomen, to the peak of my groin.

"Do you want me to leave?" he asked me as he lightly bit down on my ear, causing a small moan to escape my lips.

"No," I pathetically whined as I turned around to face him. The bathroom light cast a shadow on the side of his face, but he couldn't hide the sexy-as-fuck crooked smile of his. Suddenly, he grabbed my face, and our lips crashed together so hard the metallic taste of blood soon spread across my tongue.

Yanking his shirt up, I was stopped by his massive hands that grabbed under my ass, hoisting me up. Instinctually, I wrapped my legs around his waist as he carried us both to the bed. My fingers were threading through his hair while he pressed his face between my breasts.

"You're mine tonight. "He then dropped me to the bed, my back hitting the sheets and my body bouncing against the springs. Rising up on my elbows, I watched as Everett stepped to the bathroom, hitting the lights off before pulling his shirt over his head. I felt the dip of the bed as he knelt on the edge and swung his legs over the top of me, pinning my body down with his strong legs.

As I went to reach for his chest, he grabbed my wrists and held them firmly above my head before he started licking and kissing along my neck. I arched my back into his frame, the need for him growing with every brush of his lips across my skin.

"Everett," I moaned, the sensation of his hot lips heating my core. As soon as his name left my lips, he brought his mouth back to mine, our tongues massaging one another. As one hand continued to hold my wrists immobile, his other hand skated down my naked body until he reached the apex of my groin. He pulled back from me, leaving me wanting his lips more.

"Tell me what you want, Sloan." He breathed his words a mere whisper.

"You, I want you, please." I panted, my body wriggling beneath him desperate for his touch. His mouth came back down on mine as his fingers slowly entered my already slick pussy. He was slow, so fucking slow, as he pushed two fingers inside me—pulling them out and reentering them, making me want to scream for more friction. Pulling both fingers out, he entered a third and began making circular motions with his thumb against my throbbing clit.

"Ugh fuck," I moaned against his mouth, the pleasure building between my legs.

As his fingers worked me over into the start of an orgasm, he continued to kiss me so forcefully, my lips would no doubt be bruised by morning. A click of metal against my teeth had me startled, and I jerked my head back to meet his face. Was that a tongue ring? I know I can be ditsy at times, but I sure as hell would have noticed he had a tongue ring before. I could see the shadow of him licking his lips as he withdrew his fingers from my pussy and brought them to his mouth, sucking them clean.

"You know, baby, this has been all too easy getting you naked. You really should know better, since there's people in this world who want you dead. Better yet, you should be more aware of who you're about to fuck." His hands clamped down on my wrists hard, and the full weight of him pressed down on my hips, making it impossible to move.

"I've been meaning to introduce myself. My name is Cal. I'm sure you've heard of me by now." His lips came back down to my neck, licking up to my chin. Turning my face away, I tried to jerk away beneath his weight. He just laughed at my attempt.

"Get the fuck off me," I growled as he continued to laugh at my pathetic attempt at escaping him. His body was so heavy, so solid, my wrists started to hurt as he squeezed them harder.

"Your body tells me you do want this, you practically begged me." I jerked again. How could I have been so fucking stupid? Why didn't I see the signs before? They're fucking twins for God's sake; it's an easy mistake to make, right?

"Everett!" I screamed just as Callum's hand slapped across my mouth, the sound of his impact echoing in the room.

"Now what did you go and do that for? You're ruining the fun," he whispered in my ear before biting down hard on my ear, breaking the skin. I let out a pained scream that was muffled beneath his hand. I heard the sound of loud footsteps barreling down the hallway, and my body relaxed knowing they were coming for me.

"Remember this, little one, those boys won't be here to help you forever. I'll make sure of that." My stomach turned with the fear of anything happening to my guys, because of me.

The door burst open. Dean and Everett were standing in the doorway, their expressions horrified at the sight of Callum and me.

"I'll be seeing you around, little one." Callum then

jumped off the bed, shirtless and darted for the window. Without hesitation, he jumped through the window, glass shattering everywhere. Then he was gone.

CHAPTER 20

SLOAN

Shame and embarrassment flooded through my body as I sprung from my bed and raced to pick up my robe, quickly covering my naked, trembling body. My eyes started to sting with the threat of tears. How could I have been so fucking stupid? How did I not know it wasn't Everett? Trying to escape to the bathroom and hide my embarrassment, Everett grabbed me by the shoulders before I could make a run for it, pulling my body close to his.

"Did he hurt you? Are you okay?"

Yanking from his hold, I darted to the bathroom just in time to vomit all the contents from my stomach. I'm only thankful I, at least, made it to the toilet. Hunched over the porcelain, I feel a hand start rubbing my back as I continue to gag. My hair is suddenly pulled back from my hand that's been clenching the strands so tight my fingers hurt.

"Please, just leave me be." I say through my gags. I can't handle the shame and painful embarrassment that has now plagued my body. My muscles soon relax, but whoever is behind me has yet to make a move to leave. He's still holding my hair back and rubbing soothing circles against my skin.

"Go see if Colson has gotten home yet; we're leaving. Now."

I turn my head and meet Everett's face as he kneels behind me.

"He's in his room," I say to them. They both share a look of confusion. "He passed out in the kitchen, talking about the job he was just on, and Callum carried him to his room. I thought he was you," I choke out, tears now sliding down my face, my voice cracking as I try to hold back a sob.

I turn my head and see Dean leaving the room, but not before he gives me a look. His eyes are soft, almost apologetic as he lowers his head, turns on his heel, and leaves. I sit back from the toilet and pull my legs into my chest, wrapping my arms around them tight. I fucking hate crying. I hate feeling like someone broke me, or I'm a weak little girl, but my body betrays me as I lower my head to my knees and cry.

Everett pulls his body in close behind me, his knees boxing me in as he wraps his arms around me.

"It's okay, baby girl," Everett whispers in my ear, but he's wrong. It's not okay. I allowed a stranger to touch me, to trick me into thinking he was someone I trusted. How far would we have gone? What if I didn't notice the tongue ring? Would we have slept together? The thought of sleeping with someone who may want to kill me makes my stomach flip again. The thought alone makes me want to vomit.

"It's not okay. I let him touch me. I let him do things to me, Everett. How could I have been so fucking stupid?" Before I could rest my head back down on my knees, he captures my chin with his hand and turns my head so I have nowhere else to look, but his beautiful face.

"Sloan, don't for one second think you've done anything wrong. Callum is a master manipulator. The people who are to blame are the sorry excuse of men that are supposed to be protecting these grounds from intruders. Obviously, there will be a change in security after this." His jaw flexed at his last statement. Before I could say another word, Dean and a still very drunk Colson came into the bathroom.

"He's too drunk to understand anything we tell him right now, best wait till morning to break the news to him," Dean said, looking over his shoulder to Colson who just plopped on my bed, still not fully comprehending anything. "He's going to beat himself up about this for sure, mate." Dean tilted his head towards Colson as he spoke to the both of us. He shook his head in agreement, a look of worry quickly showing through his stoic face, but it disappeared almost instantly.

"Get your things, mate, along with Colson's if you

don't mind. I'm going to help Sloan pack and text the jet to be ready in an hour. We're leaving as soon as possible." With that Everett stood from the floor and reached out his hand to help me up as well. Dean nodded once and grabbed Colson from underneath his arm, hoisting him up as if he weighed nothing at all. Then the two of them disappeared down the hall, leaving Everett and me alone once more.

"Where are we going?" I asked quietly, still ashamed of myself, because honestly who wouldn't be after what I did? Everett led me to the bed and ushered me to sit, while he pulled out his phone and started typing a mile a minute. Seconds later, one of the guards, or supposed to be guards, came into the room, looking as if someone had just shot his puppy.

"Yes, sir," the man said, voice shaky.

"Take the others and leave. You obviously can't do your jobs and allow anyone to fucking walk into the house. What good are you? Get the others and fucking leave. You're no longer needed." Everett's voice was pure venom as the guard cowered at his words. He knew he had fucked up. In their defense, I thought he was Everett as well. They are more than identical twins; they are a perfect copy and paste of one another. Everything, and I mean everything, about them is similar. Their frames, their gestures, their voices. The only way I caught on was the tongue ring, so how could the guards have known it was Callum unless he kissed each and every one of them also?

Glancing over at the guard, whose posture was ramrod straight and his face looking more defeated with every word Everett spat at him, I gave him an apologetic expression. Just as Everett finished berating the guard, I had to speak up.

"I thought he was you too. I couldn't tell the difference by appearance alone. If he's worthless, then so am I." I notice the guard step back one step towards the door, almost waiting for his boss to explode. Everett's face is somber as he looks back to me.

"You two are practically a reflection of one another. I'm sorry, Everett, but I don't think you should be so hard on them."

Everett turns and steps in front of me as he grabs my hand, lifting me from the bed.

"Yes, yes, I can be mad, love. This is their job; they're trained at the highest level. For them to make a careless mistake and not be on their toes, almost ended in chaos, more than it already was. There are ways to tell us apart." Everett brushed his hair back exposing his tattoos on his temple that are indeed different from Callum's. I should have noticed that as well.

"Grab the others, pack the cars, and get it ready to depart in the next hour. We're going to the airstrip." The guard nodded and left the room. I lowered my head, thinking about visible differences between the two that I missed. Apart from the tattoos on their temples and Callum's tongue ring, I couldn't remember anything that could help me tell them apart. Everett must have seen my thoughts racing because as he went to the dresser to grab my clothes to pack, he said, "Callum has a scar above his left eyebrow; it's small, but when you look for it, you can see it looks almost like a fish hook. He got it when we were in training. We were sparring and he couldn't dodge my knife, and I clipped his eyebrow. He also has a birthmark on the side of his neck, the right side I believe, is a little larger than a quarter."

He paused as he fetched a bag out of the closet and started filling it with my clothes. "One more thing, he has a burn mark on the top of his right hand." He sighed under his breath.

"He got the scar at Stone Fortress. He was seen trying to escape the training room and, well, his punishment was one to make an example out of all of us." My face fell, thinking about the lives they've lived. I've heard nothing positive from their childhood, only horror stories that leave my chest aching for them. Yet, my childhood was no sunshine and rainbows either. I guess you could call us all damaged goods. Then it dawned on me.

"Wait, Callum was at Stone Fortress too? Was he a Shadow as well?" Everett stopped packing, his hands still clutching a shirt of mine, his head lowered to the floor. He froze for a moment before standing from his knees and cracking his neck as he stood to his full height.

"Yes, he was once a Shadow," Everett admitted, his face hard and unreadable.

"A damn good one at that." Dean's voice came from the doorway, startling me and interrupting the stare off between Everett and me. The room was silent for a moment, the three of us just looking at one another, until a cold breeze had me shiver and looking to the now broken window. The cool window blew hard as the curtains fanned into the room.

"Here, get dressed, we need to leave." Everett zipped up my bag and nodded to the clothes he had lain out for me. Jeans, a dark sweater, and my bra and panty set. I started dressing when Everett spoke again. "I'm going to get my bag together and will meet you both in the car." He gave me one last look and turned towards Dean at the door.

"Colson's in the car already, passed out in the back."

Everett just nodded and headed down the hall. Pulling up my jeans and buttoning the bottoms, I tried latching my bra but was fumbling over the clasps.

"Here let me," Dean said, twisting his finger to have me turn around for him. I did as he said, and as his fingers brushed across my skin, I shivered again—his fingers as cold as ice.

"Sorry, baby girl, I just came back from outside, loading up Colson. It's fucking freezing tonight." He finished, and I turned to face him, the feeling of embarrassment creeping back into my stomach. I turned my face from his.

"Don't do that," he said, making me turn back to him.

"Do what?"

"Shy away from us as if you think we're mad at you. He's a master at his art, and his specialty is interrogation. We all have a skill that trumps all other skills. His is communication. That's what makes him so dangerous." He brushed a loose strand of hair from my face before continuing. "So don't think for one second we could ever be mad at you for something he did, something he tricked you into doing." He leaned down so his eyes were level with mine and pressed his forehead to mine.

"Remember, love, you've been thrown into this world against your will. Nothing will ever be your fault." Leaving it at that, he placed a gentle kiss on my forehead and helped me into my sweater. After I slipped into my shoes, he threaded his fingers through mine and we both made our way down the hall, down the stairs, and to the garage.

Everett was already there, waiting for us on his phone, along with a handful of guards that all looked to have been thoroughly scorned at.

As we climbed into the G-class, Everett hung up the phone with whomever he was speaking to and settled into the driver's seat, while Dean and I climbed in the back with Colson. One of the guards, one I've never seen before, sat ready in the passenger seat, laptop open and his fingers typing away.

"We've finally reached a contact within Shem's close circle. Looks like they have a location where you can meet with Sloan's siblings. They're in Ireland," the guard informs us all as he continues typing on his computer, not even lifting his head as he speaks.

CHAPTER 21

SLOAN

We arrived at an airstrip roughly thirty minutes after leaving the mansion. We boarded a small private jet that was fully equipped with a white tiled bathroom, shower, a bedroom with a king bed, fully stocked bar, and luxury chocolate-colored seats that were more comfortable than any La-Z-Boy I'd ever sat in.

The guys loaded up all the bags, along with a still passed out Colson, laying him on the bed fully clothed. I sat next to him for a moment before we took off, watching him as he twitched and groaned in his sleep. He sounded like he was dreaming about something, and I wondered if I should wake him, fearing he was having a nightmare. I decided against it, wanting him to get as much rest as he could, especially given how drunk he was.

I left the bedroom and sat in one of the reclining

seats, buckling myself in. The guys were talking to the pilot and reviewing a map of sorts. I looked around the plane and noticed a fluffy black sherpa blanket folded up in a small cubby to the left of my seat below the window. Pulling it out I covered myself up and reclined my seat some, getting comfortable, not truly knowing how long of a flight we were in for.

I ended up falling asleep before we even took off, exhaustion taking hold of me. I woke to the sound of the guys talking about the incident with Callum. I kept my eyes closed and decided to just listen to their conversation as I stayed curled up in my chair.

"The fucker carried me to my room, fucking carried me like a drunken fool. I allowed this to happen. If I'd been awake, I would have known it was him. I let her be in danger, mate. This is all my fault," Colson said, his voice groggy and full of guilt.

"Listen, mate, no one blames you for what happened. How the fuck he was able to sneak in with that many of our guys watching the house is beyond me. We're concerned about your health. How many jobs have you taken since the incident at the warehouse?" Dean asked, his voice right behind me. I guessed he was sitting in the recliner that was back-to-back with mine.

There was a pause, Colson not answering right away. "To be honest, I'm not entirely sure. Maybe twelve or thirteen."

There was another long pause, only the sound of

the jet engine rumbling through. Colson had been busy, but I hadn't realized just how many jobs he'd been working on. Surely that would take a toll on anyone, especially with that line of work.

"Listen, mate. I think it may be time for you to take a small break. Get your head straight again before accepting more jobs," Everett says with a heavy sigh. "I'll let them know you're in need of some time, for personal reasons or some shit. Anyone of us would need time after the shit you've been seeing lately." The sound of ice clicking the side of a tumbler filled the small space. Everett was no doubt drinking.

"How could I have let this happen?" Colson's voice was so low I almost didn't hear him. "What if he would have done something worse to her? What if he took her right after putting my drunk ass to bed? I know he's your brother, mate, but when I see him next, I'm going to kill him." His words were a promise on his tongue.

"Get in line," Dean scoffed.

"He may be my blood, but he is no brother to me."

Just then the pilot announced over the intercom that we were landing in the next twenty minutes, and I decided to make it known I was no longer asleep.

Stretching in my chair, I yawned and sat up, turning to see all three of my guys sitting in their own recliner chairs. Dean sat right behind me, Colson sat in front of Dean, and Everett to Colson's right, his legs stretched wide as he held his tumbler to his temple.

"Where are we exactly?" I asked looking out the window to see a vast forest beneath us, the sun peeking out behind the clouds. A sheen of fog blanketed the tops of the trees, making the whole area look like the beginning of a horror film. I could see a channel of water in the distance, stretching as far as the eye could see.

"Is that the English Channel?" I asked as I turned my gaze back to the three of them.

"It is, love. We'll be on the outskirts of a town called Arundale; it's near the channel. Our estate is off in a secluded area within the forest," Everett said as he spun his tumbler around in his hand, making the ice clink against the crystal again. This was a habit of his I'd picked up on. Not a nervous habit, but one that gave his hands something to do when he had a lot on his mind.

We started to descend closer to the woodland area, and off in the distance I noticed a small landing strip. It must have been a private airport, because the only indication it was an airport at all was, of course, the landing strip, but also a small hangar that housed only two other small jets. A large, black SUV waited at the end of the runway with two men wearing black clothing and standing on either side of the vehicle. Very James Bond-ish, really.

The four of us were quiet as the jet landed and pulled up near the vehicle. Unbuckling as soon as the jet came to a stop, I stood up and stretched my arms above my head, trying to get my muscles awake from being curled up in an awkward sleeping position. Everett and Dean made their way to the door, which they unlatched and lowered before grabbing our bags and heading to the vehicle to load up.

"Baby girl," Colson's voice was a mere whisper, but his hand brushed against my lower back getting my attention. I spun to face him. His hair was draped around his face, dark circles prominent beneath his eyes, and his once vibrant eyes were now dull and glazed over with a sheen of water. He was hungover. I was sure of it.

"I can't apologize enough for what happened last night. I shouldn't have been that way; none of this should have happened." His eyes never left mine, his sincerity evident as he places his hand on my cheek, gently brushing my jaw line. I close my eyes at the gesture, warmth radiating from where he touches me.

"Please, don't say sorry," I whisper, my eyes fluttering open to see he's a mere inch from my face, our noses almost touching.

"I could never forgive myself if something happened to you, especially something I could've stopped." He kisses me then, his lips soft and gentle as he presses his body into mine. I hold tight to his shirt, pulling him closer as if our bodies could morph into one and still, we wouldn't be close enough.

"Right, vehicles ready, let's go you two." Dean's

voice breaks our hold, and Colson's lips, to my protest, disappear from mine. Colson looks down at me, giving me a smile that doesn't quite reach his eyes, grabbing my hand as he leads us out of the jet and to the awaiting SUV.

The two guards, whom I guess work with the guys, drive us deeper and deeper into the woodland area. I have yet to see any town, home, person, or even an animal since we started driving.

We've been driving for roughly forty-five minutes, and I'm about to ask how much longer we have, when we turn off the road onto a gravel driveway. The driveway is not far off the road itself, because I quickly spot a rusty iron gate up ahead. The gate is massive, I mean super freaking massive, and it looks like the entrance to an old manor you would see in a vampire movie or something. There is no keypad or intercom system to open the gate, but I see the driver click a button that's attached to the sun visor and the gate suddenly opens.

The screech of the iron gate opening gives me the chills as I peer through the windows, anxiously awaiting where we are going. The driver slowly accelerates down the driveway that's lined with thick dense forest on either side. We drive another mile or so down the driveway, when a castle-like mansion starts to come into view.

My jaw drops as we pull up to exactly that, a fucking castle. Not a castle like Cinderella's or Snow

White's; this is a castle where the villains would live. A castle that Dracula would have or Maleficent. The castle looks old, ancient even, but well taken care of. The structure has the traditional four pillars, one on each corner with gargoyles perched on each one. Each one scarier than the next.

The difference with this castle that makes it so eerie is the fact that the stone itself is the darkest of blacks. Since the windows have sharp black iron bars lining the frames, I expected to see a moat with alligators or some shit.

The driveway turns into a half circle leading right up to the arched doorway that looks more like a prison door to a dungeon than a home. This place is anything but welcoming, the cold exterior gives off the feeling of danger and that you should run if you want to live. As if he can read my thoughts, Everett takes my hand in his and says, "Never judge a book by its cover. Come, let me show you." He opens the car door and leads me out into the cool evening air. I shiver as the wind creeps into my sweater, chilling me to the bone. He brings us to the front where the double doors are crafted into an arch, two iron circle handles hang on either door. However, when he goes to open the door, he doesn't grab on to the iron circle. Instead, he places his palm on a scanner I didn't see before. The scanner is off to the side of the door, on the wall adjacent to the door itself.

The scanner then identifies Everett's unique handprint, and a loud clunk comes from the inside of the door. The door slowly starts to open inward, creaking as the wood scraps against the stone flooring. Everett pulls me inside, and I immediately understand the meaning of "never judge a book by its cover." What the fuck is this place?

CHAPTER 22

SLOAN

When I tell you my jaw dropped, it flat out disconnected from my face and shattered on the floor. Dracula's castle turned out to be Martha Stewart's country home. The inside was full of neutral earthy colors, far from the dark and eerie look of its shell. Walking into the foyer, I saw a massive plush carpet that extended to the sitting area. It was front and center as you stepped through the archway. In the center of the sitting area were two large white sofas facing each other, and in between sat around white marble coffee table. On the table sat a small sculpture of half a man's face. It looked to be ceramic and all white.

At the end of the living space was a floor-to-ceiling fireplace that was, again, all white marble that had swirls of gold spiraling up to the ceiling. Their other house was mostly a black and gold interior, but this castle had a lot of white and beige furniture. It made the room feel so warm and inviting. I didn't notice I had started walking into the castle, jaw still ajar, as I absorbed my new surroundings and the sheer beauty of this place.

Turning around, I saw the guys, all three, standing in the foyer and staring at me intently.

"What?" I asked, picking up my jaw and fidgeting with the end sleeves of my sweater. Everett pulled out one of his hands from his pockets and brushed his thumb along his jaw, a crooked smile on his face.

"Nothing at all, just watching your eyes light up in a way I've never seen before."

I played with the hem of my sweater, not knowing how to respond.

"What do you think, baby girl?" Dean asked from behind Everett, his body leaning against the doorway and arms crossed over his chest.

"It's not what I was expecting, if I'm being honest. The outside is, well, very deceiving. But this"—I waved my arms at the castle—"This is the most beautiful and breathtaking place I've ever stepped foot in. I feel like I'm inside Cinderella's castle." I turned as I spoke, continuing to take in this seriously impressive place they can call one of their homes.

"Would you like to see the rest of it, love?" Colson's voice was low, and I could tell he was still beating himself up about the whole incident. I turned to look at him. He was standing to the side of Everett, his long hair now in his usual messy bun, and his hands hanging loosely from his pockets.

"Please," I said to him, giving him a small smile as I reached out my hand.

"Take your time. Dean and I are going to bring in the bags and then take care of something with the others." With that he and Dean turned to leave and headed out the door. I threaded my fingers through Colson's, and we began our tour through the castle.

This place was more than I could've ever imagined it would be. The kitchen was so grand, with a massive island that was the centerpiece of the room. The glass cabinets allowed their contents to be on full display. Each cabinet housed glass dishes that were perfectly lined up, one by one. The refrigerator was designed to look like a cabinet as well, white with gold handles. The other appliances were all state of the art and looked as if they'd never been used.

Leaving the kitchen, we ventured into a room that was off the kitchen, and made up of only windows, even the ceiling was windows. It was stunning. Another sitting area, but this one had large white chairs with an ottoman for each chair. It felt like a study or maybe a reading room. In the corner of the room was a small bookshelf that had a few books here and there stacked sporadically between a few decorations. I could already tell without even looking at the rest of the castle that this would be my favorite room.

Upstairs there were many, many rooms. Most of the rooms had a bed, closet, and private bathroom. There was also an office, theater room, a billiards room, a lounge room, a sauna, and a fitness room. But I still hadn't seen the rooms designated for each of the guys.

"Where do you guys' sleep?" I asked.

"We sleep on the opposite wing. Here, follow me."

I should have known there would be a whole other wing. He led me down the hallway, which felt like it was half the size of a fitness track, until we got to the end and then turned down another hallway. This one was shorter, and I guessed this was where their rooms were.

Colson led me to the first room, opening the door and ushering me to enter first. He flipped the light switch on, and I was surprised to see windows lining the whole back of the room, overlooking the dense forest.

"Oh my God! This is beautiful."

The room was large, but had barely any furniture, so it felt even larger. A king-sized bed stood opposite the windows, allowing for the person to enjoy the view while lying comfortably in bed. There was a bathroom off to the side and double doors, which I guessed led to the closet. There were two cushioned chairs with a small table between the two that sat at the corner of the room near the windows.

I walk over to the large windows and stare out

into the forest. It's dusk out, a small amount of fog had started to settle between the many trees. There's a slight breeze, making the leaves shift on their branches, and the darkness of the sun's departure has started to vanish within the tall trees.

"This room's mine." He's standing behind me, his warm breath feathering my neck as we both look out into the trees. "It's calming, isn't it? Watching mother nature and her beauty, her strength and sheer size. Makes me feel small again. Like I'm just a pawn on her game board and I'm not in control of my own environment. I'm just a life source, and she's the master of it all."

His words stun me. I've never heard Colson like this before. He's usually the playful, joking one, yet he just described our earth in the most serene way. I lean back into his hard body and grab his arms to wrap around my waist.

"Remind me to thank her for bringing me to you." I lean my head back on his shoulder, and I can feel his body relax against mine. "I'm glad we're here; it's peaceful."

He places a kiss on my head and tightens his hold on my waist. "This is my favorite place in the world, love. I'm happy we get to share it with you."

I turn to face him and place my hands in his chest as I step in closer to him. "Thank you. I love it here." I kiss his full lips, and I can feel his tension melt away as he kisses me back. He cups my face with his hands and pushes me until my back is pressed against the window. The window is cold from the outdoors, and I shiver at the sensation as my sweater rises up, leaving my back exposed to the cool glass.

"I'm so sorry, Sloan, for letting him touch you and manipulate you the way he did. I should've protected you. I should've….done my job." His lips brushed mine as he spoke. His words were an apology as he grinded his body into mine, igniting a fire in my core. I hadn't been with Colson in a while. Him being gone more recently had left us with little time together. My body was craving his touch.

His hands released my face and started their way down the length of my body and stopped at the back of my thighs as he hoisted my body off the floor. Instinctively, I wrapped my legs around his waist and steadied my hands on his shoulders. He continued to kiss me as he spun us around and walked over to one of the chairs in the corner of his room. He gently lowered us to the cushion as he perched my ass on his lap, the undeniable bulge pressing against my now restrictive pants.

"I've missed you," I said. Both of our breathing was becoming more jagged as we devoured one another.

"I've never left, nor will I ever leave you."

I kiss him harder, the clothing between us smothering me as my body grinds on top of his. Just then a knock at the door breaks me from my bliss, and I turn my head to see Everett in the doorway.

"Where would you like me to put your bag, love?" he asks as I turn to look at him. I hadn't seen my room yet, or rather the room that would be my designated room for the time spent here.

"Uhm, I...I don't know. Whatever room I guess you want me to use." I shrugged with confusion and turned back to Colson, meeting his eyes. He licked his bottom lip, and it took all I had not to do the same to his lip. I really, really missed him.

"You have three to choose from. Mine, Dean's, or Colson's."

I cocked my head toward Everett, making me look no doubt like a confused puppy. Just as I was about to speak, Everett beat me to it.

"You're no longer going to have a room of your own. You'll stay with either Dean, Colson, or me every night. This place is safe; there's no denying that. But I would feel more comfortable if one of us has eyes on you at all times. Especially at night."

I was no longer fighting him on this. I liked my own space, but I wasn't going to deny that when I was alone, bad things always seemed to find me.

"She's with me tonight, mate. We have some catching up to do." Colson broke the silence, and I was glad he did. I hated to verbally choose between the three of them, but I really, really needed Colson tonight, and from the way his jeans pitched beneath me, I guessed he needed me as well.

"Right," Everett said with a sigh and a hint of jealousy. "You're mine tomorrow, baby girl, so you better get some rest." My heart raced with his promise, and I turned to watch Everett leave, closing the door behind him. How did I become the luckiest bitch on the planet? I smiled within as I silently thanked the heavens for these three insanely gorgeous men I get to call mine.

CHAPTER 23

SLOAN

His fingers grabbed the hem of my sweater and slowly started to lift the soft fabric up my abdomen. Colson's fingers were feather soft as they brushed across my skin and lifted the sweater up over my head. Lips as soft as butter met my chest as he placed sweet kisses across the mounds of my breasts. His fingers found the hooks of my bra and, like magic, he unclasped the straps, all while his lips never left my skin.

Freeing my breasts, he tossed the bra somewhere in the room, his lips now reaching my nipples as he kissed and sucked on one. I leaned my head back in utter bliss as his mouth explored my breasts. Arching my back, I pressed my chest to him even further, my body greedily wanting more of his mouth on me.

This chair was suddenly starting to make me feel constricted. As if hearing my thoughts, Colson's hands found my ass once more and lifted me as he raised himself up and then led me to the bed. He gently laid me on the bed. The covers were silky smooth and soft as a cloud. I leaned on my elbows and brushed my fingers along the comforter as I watched Colson lift his shirt over his head. His jeans hung low on his hips, his muscular frame on full display.

He then unbuttoned his jeans, making my mouth water, but stopped before reaching the zipper.

"Let me take these off for you, since you won't be needing them tonight." He grabbed the waist of my pants and pulled them down in one quick pull. Along with my pants, my panties followed with them, Colson not missing to grab them as well. I was completely exposed to him now, his eyes lighting up for the first time in a while.

"Fuck, sweetheart, you're utter perfection." He groaned, placing his hands on the bed and prowling his way up to my face. "I don't deserve you." His nose brushed over mine, our lips just barely touching.

"Stop saying stuff like that. No more apologizing. What's in the past is in the past."

He gave me a mischievous smile before replying. "Well then, I was going to apologize one last time, but if you're sure." He cupped my pussy with his hand making me gasp at the sudden touch. His warm hand pressed firm against my sensitive folds, which were now throbbing for more.

"Well, maybe one more apology won't hurt." I moaned at his touch, my core almost hurting at the need for him to touch me more. He chuckled at my plea and slowly began to kiss his way down my neck, over my chest, and down my abdomen to the apex of my groin. I let out a sharp breath as his warm lips kissed the inside of my thighs.

I looked down, my legs lay open with his hands wrapped tightly around my thighs, his eyes closed, and his lips sent shockwaves throughout my body. He hummed against my folds, and I fell back to the bed, my eyes rolling back into my head as sheer pleasure ignited the fire deep in my stomach.

"Colson," I whimpered, just as his tongue licked between my folds and swirled around my clit. Fireworks exploded in my head as my hands gripped the blanket beneath me. My whole body tensed as his tongue continued to lick and suck me in the most delicious of apologies I'd ever received. The orgasm within was building fast as Colson introduced a finger into me, and my legs twitched as I panted with need.

I moaned and jerked as my orgasm was about to implode, and just as I was about to see stars, he was gone. My body suddenly felt empty as I lifted my head just in time to see Colson line himself up with my entrance and slowly push the head of his cock inside me. He grabbed my thighs and pulled me closer to him, fully seeding himself inside my needy pussy. He let out a deep growl just as a sharp gasp spilled from my mouth.

"Fuck, baby girl, I've missed you." He started at a slow pace, pulling himself out and then pushing all the way in, my pussy clenching around his thick cock. As he continued to pump into me, he reached his thumb between my legs and pushed just enough on my sensitive clit, which had me seeing stars. My orgasm was so strong that my body convulsed beneath him as waves of pleasure swirled throughout my body.

Just as I was coming down from my climax, my body was suddenly flipped over, Colson's hands grabbing my hips and hiking my ass in the air. He placed his hand on the dip of my back, making me arch further into him. When he pushed his cock inside me, he reached a whole different angle, which had me screaming into the blanket and Colson groaning as he started pumping once more.

I could feel another orgasm building, and I gripped the blankets once again as I focused on the pleasure that was about to erupt inside me for the second time. As my face was pressed into the bed, I felt his hand curl around my neck and squeeze ever so gently as his pace picked up.

"Yes, baby, scream for me again." His voice was deep as he groaned through his own pleasure. "Come for me again; be a good little girl." Colson's cock started to twitch inside me, and I knew he was about to come when he squeezed my neck a little harder.

"I'm almost there," I pleaded, just when I felt a finger come down on my clit once again, and that was all I need. I'm spiraling off into another bone-shattering orgasm, with Colson chasing his right after. He pushed his cock so deep inside, his hands now on my hips with a bruising hold. His cock was twitching inside me, his seed dripping down my thighs along with my own pleasure.

Staying fully inside me, he glides his hands down my back reaching the back of my neck and squeezing me as he lifts my body off the bed and flush against his chest. His long fingers wrap around my neck as I rest my head against his shoulder and look up to his beautiful face.

"You're my light, baby girl, a light that blinds out the darkness and reassures me there is still good in this evil world." His cock slowly slides out of me, and my body immediately wants him back inside. "I want more," he whispers this last bit, and I close my eyes as goosebumps pepper my skin at the words.

"Then take more." My words are breathy, our bodies stuck together as we both pant with desire for one another. Colson turns my face to his and kisses me with the force of a hurricane, or bodies crashing to one another, and I can tell tonight is going to be a very, very restless night. Colson and I have a lot of catching up to do...

CHAPTER 24

DEAN

Everett's been able to contact a member of Shem's inner circle that has agreed to meet with us. To say I'm uneasy with this idea would be an understatement, and by the way Everett is pacing back and forth in the office; he feels the same. We've both been in the office since arriving at the castle, Colson and Sloan having "their time" while we continued our search for the twins and now Callum as well. Whatever involvement that fucker has with Sloan we have yet to determine. Whatever it is, he's most certainly already signed his death warrant for what he did to Sloan.

I crack my neck and stretch out my legs, trying to get comfortable in the oversized chair I'm sitting in. My computer is open over my lap, and my eyes are quickly becoming heavy with exhaustion. I've been in contact with the organization and the few tech guys that've been helping us with our search to try and get more information about this contact we've managed to find.

"It was too easy find this contact, mate; something doesn't feel right," I admit to Everett, who's still pacing in the office and clenching his crystal glass that's been empty now for the past fifteen minutes.

"Right," he says, agreeing with me, but not really knowing what to do other than to follow through with the meeting. The contact agreed to meet as long as we met in Ireland at a remote location he would provide to us twenty-four hours prior to the meet. Yeah, sounds shady as fuck, if you ask me.

"What have the guys found out about this contact?" he asked me. I look back down to my computer but already know the answer.

"Nothing really. Their name is William. He's been working with Shem all his life, as well as his father before him. He's aware of Sloan and how Shem has been searching for his granddaughter to bring her into the business. That's all pretty vague—an identity easily created if you ask me." My stomach turns as more thoughts of how this could all go wrong start swirling in my head.

"Fuck, mate. How the fuck is this all connected to Callum? Why the fuck is he involved? That's what's keeping me up at night, Dean. That fucking snake and his tricks. When I see him, he's dead. Should have been dead a long time ago." Everett finally sits in a chair identical to mine and leans his head back all the way, letting out a frustrated sigh. Then he did something he's only ever done once in our lifetime together. He asked me what we should do.

"Listen, Everett, this whole meeting sounds fucked and sketchy as shit, but to be honest, I will do anything to ensure her safety. And from the looks of it, so would you."

"She's our savior—the spark we needed to survive this fucked-up life we live," Colson's voice had me turning to the office door. He was pulling on a T-shirt and looking all types of freshly fucked by our girl.

"Couldn't agree more, mate," Everett said as I nodded in agreement. Colson came in and laid down on the sofa in the office, placing his arm across his face while he rested his head on the other.

We all sat quiet for a long while, all of us lost in our thoughts. Sloan was our job at first, a simple snatch and deliver. It should have been a quick paycheck and that's all, so how did we get here? How has this woman latched on to all our hearts and put us all in a choke hold? We are killers; we do our jobs and move on to the next fucked-up individual that's been so lucky to have a kill order placed on their head. Yet we're playing Sherlock Holmes, trying to protect the woman who unknowingly saved our souls from the abyss of darkness we've all been falling deeper and deeper into.

For the past two to three years now, Everett, Colson, and myself have started to lose what makes a man a good man. We've been utterly consumed with the jobs we've been tasked with, and while we've never had an issue with killing "bad people," we've started to lose the emotional connection that every human being needs to survive. Rather, the three of us have become zombies to our work. Where we once held emotions such as happiness, desire, and even love, has now become a distant memory. Until she came into our lives.

Emotions are truly a complex force if you think about it. How can a feeling change the course of how you act or behave throughout the course of our lives? A question I've yet to find an answer to. But when these emotions are absent, the feeling of being numb is frightening for those looking on the outside. You start to do and act in a way where you no longer care about the outcomes or consequences. You become numb, a vessel that's robotic in the way you move and act. This has been our lives for the past few years, and if it weren't for Sloan, we would all soon have become permanent occupants of the abyss, forever lost in the dark and never finding the way to the light again.

"We've lost ourselves. We've become what we always feared we would be. Zombies to the world outside of the organization, the perfect tools to be used for murder. We've let The Shadows become our identities, our only identities." Everett's words are a boulder to my chest.

"When did we let this happen to us?" Colson says from beneath his arm that is draped loosely over his face. I close the computer on my lap and lean my head back to the cushion, a dull headache starting to throb between my eyes. Again, the room is quite the realization of who and what we've become seeping into the deepest parts of our souls.

I'm not a big believer that everything happens for a reason, but by the state of the three of us, I do believe Sloan was created for not just one of us but the three of us. She single-handedly crawled into the chasm of darkness and guided three broken souls out of the sticky black tar that's been holding us back from reaching the light.

"We are going to the meeting," I say, breaking the silence. "We go to the meeting and find the remaining bit of family she has and give her the life she's always deserved. That's the least we can do for her." Out of the corner of my eye, I see Colson's arm raise from his face, his gaze heating my face. I look over to Everett, who's also staring at me, and nods his approval.

"She may have been brought into this mess unwillingly, but there's a reason she's here. She's saving us, mates, from ourselves." With Everett's words, we decided as a team to go to Ireland, for our girl.

CHAPTER 25

SLOAN

The three of them stand at the door with several bags scattered around them on the floor. Huge black duffle bags each full to max capacity with Lord knows what. Colson is kneeling at one of his bags shuffling items around, as Everett is on the phone with what sounds to be the airstrip. He's been scheduling their jet to head to Ireland today, and from what it sounds like, this will be a night flight. It's roughly four in the evening now, and Everett just confirmed a five o'clock takeoff time.

"Why do you look like someone just killed your dog, baby girl?" Dean asks from behind me. I didn't hear him approach and his sudden presence startled me.

"Shit, Dean, you scared me."

Dean spun me around, his hands on my waist as he brought me into his large frame. Looking down at me, he rubbed his thumb down my cheek. I closed my eyes at the touch and inhaled a deep breath. Dean's scent hit my nostrils, and I smelled every bit of sandalwood and bourbon. I lay my head on his chest, taking in more of him. His hand instinctively wrapped around me, squeezing me gently and making me feel utterly safe in his hold.

"So, are you going to tell me what's on your mind, love?"

I sighed against his hold, anxiety bubbling in my stomach at the fear of them leaving. They can handle themselves; there's no denying that, but this is the Irish mob we are talking about. I can't imagine they play fair in the game of life. Something tells me this is not the right move; I fear the worst for my guys, and I can't stomach having another warehouse event.

"Something feels off with you guys leaving," I admit, my arms squeezing him a little tighter. I feel the rise and fall of his chest against my face as if sighing heavily himself.

"The quicker we leave, the quicker we can return to you. Nothing to be worried about; we are trained for this." His words are no less satisfying, as my fear still swirls in my gut. "Just try not to give Cain and Stone too much trouble while we're away, okay?"

I lift my head quickly, meeting his mischievous smile. "Cain and Stone, as in my babysitters from before?" I asked, feeling stupid to think they would leave me alone while they were gone.

"I prefer to call us guardians, rather than babysitters. Right, Stone?" Cain's voice comes from the doorway as he and Stone walk in, each carrying a small bag for themselves.

"What, not happy to see us? And to think I brought popcorn." Stone's joking comment has me internally chuckling.

"Don't forget why you're here. Anything happens to her, and it will be your head. I don't want a hair out of place on her head, you got that?" Dean's voice was almost demonic as he threatened the two. I've only had the pleasure of being babysat by the two meatheads once before, but I feel oddly safe with them both here, like two overprotective big brothers.

With his hands in the air, Cain replies, "No worries, mate, she'll be safe. No need to go all Jack the Ripper on us."

That wasn't the smartest thing to say to Dean; he already had murderous intent written all over his handsome face.

"Jack the Ripper will look like fucking Mother Teresa after I'm done with you if she's hurt. Keep that in mind."

Cain and Stone just nod, and a veil of seriousness drapes over their faces. They are in Shadows mode now, no fucking around.

The two guards make their way past the two of us and into the sitting area. From the looks of them knowing where to go, I take it they've been here before. I watch as they leave. A second later, I feel Dean's hand on my face once more. Drawing my attention back to him, he lowers his face to mine. When his lips touch mine, my whole body relaxes. The heat of his lips making me melt into his mouth as I kiss him back.

"Just, please come back in one piece," I say, holding back the sudden tears that threaten to spill as the sting in my eyes grow. A sharp slap to my ass has me yelping, as I spin around to deliver a swift slap to Colson's chest.

"Damn it, Colson, that's going to leave a mark," I say to him as his smile grows wider.

"That's right, marking my territory, baby girl."

I can't help but smile as he gives me a crooked smile. I wrap my arms around his neck giving him a crushing hug as well. The love I have for them all is crippling whenever we're apart. They've embedded themselves into my soul deeper than I thought possible. Starting off being my captors, to becoming the keepers to my heart and my body. I've never felt the feeling of love before. If the flood of emotions that have taken hold of me since meeting these men is any indication of what love feels like, you could say I've delivered my heart to them on a silver platter.

Everett ends his call and steps over to where Dean, Colson, and I are standing. As soon as I release my arms from Colson's neck, Everett grabs my waist, hoisting me into his arms. Wrapping my legs around his slim waist, I hold on to him like a koala, not wanting to let either of them leave.

"Be safe, please, be safe," I whisper into Everett's ear, his hold on me tightening.

"Always do, love." His whisper back is reassuring, but still, I'm uneasy. I kiss his neck as he starts walking us to the office, his hands now clenching my ass as we both disappear into the office on the main level. Setting me on the desk, he pulls back from me, and his eyes are piercing as he cups my face.

"What have you done to me, Sloan?" Everett speaks in a hushed whisper. I'm unsure how to answer him. I'm not entirely sure what he means. He must see my confusion because he speaks again, "I've never cared for anyone else in my entire life besides those two blokes." He tilts his head to Colson and Dean. "But here you are." He pauses as his thumbs brush across my cheeks, his eyes never once leaving mine. "You've made falling in love as easy as taking a breath. My heart is yours, Sloan, all of my heart, now and forever. I'm not going anywhere and neither are you. I've said it before and I'll say it again, you're mine."

I missed everything he said after he spoke the word "love." The heat that's raised up my neck has now started to reach my cheeks, and when I open my mouth, nothing comes out.

"What he means to say is, he loves you; we all love you, baby girl," Dean chimes in from behind Everett, and now I'm surely about to faint. Never has another soul said those words to me in my life. My mother, my father, neither have ever uttered those words. My eyes start stinging, and as hard as I try, I can't stop the tear that slides down my cheek.

"I-I…umm…no one has ever said that to me before," I admit, my heart racing so fast I swear they can hear it beating. My palms have started to sweat, and I can't help but grab on to Everett for another hug. My body shaking against his, I say, "I love you too. I love all of you. Please don't go." I'm fully crying now, my tears flowing freely down my cheeks. "Please, just stay here with me, don't go." I pull back from Everett, his hold on my waist easing up as I see Colson and Dean reach either side of Everett.

Colson hops on the desk beside me, placing his hand around my neck and pulling me to his chest. I hold on to him tight and kiss his neck as a sob escapes my throat.

"It's not a goodbye, love; it's a see you later. We'll be fine, I promise." Colson promises in my ear. "By the way, I love you, too, sweetheart." He kisses my cheek and hops back off the desk, taking up his spot beside Everett. Looking at the three of my guys, I can tell neither of them want to leave. Their faces are having a hard time hiding their concern, each one holding their stress in the deep groves of their foreheads.

"Can I have a moment with our girl?" Dean asks the guys, both of them turning their heads, to give him a look.

"Don't be scared, mate, just tell her you love her too. There's no denying we're all fucking in love with each other," Colson says as he pulls the elastic out of his hair, letting his golden locks fall to his shoulders. Chuckling to myself, I watch Colson quickly redo his man bun at a rapid pace. He'd blow most girls out of the water with how fast he can make his bun. I've seen some girls struggle to wrap their hair in a pony-tail for fuck's sake.

"Get fucked, mate, and while you're at it, get a damn haircut." Dean's tone was playful but neverthe-less Colson got the hint, flipping Dean off as he made his way to the foyer.

"Don't be too long; we're on a schedule." Everett leaned in, grabbing the back of my head and pulling me to him, giving me a bruising kiss. Fuck, I didn't want him to go. I didn't want any of them to leave. "You'll be safe with Cain and Stone. Just always stay alert. Trust no one, and we'll be back in two days' time, at the most." He kissed me again before releasing my head and saying one last time, "I love you, Sloan."

I watched as he left the office and reentered the foyer. I looked at Dean, his face etched with an expression I couldn't decipher. He made his way in front of me, parting my legs so he could stand even closer to me. Dean's large hands lay on my thighs as he slowly slid them up to the hinge of my leg, danger-ously close to my throbbing core. The sensation of his touch caused my muscles to flex beneath him.

"Baby girl," Dean cooed, pressing his forehead to mine. "Never in my time on this earth have I ever said I love you to a woman, not even my mother, but I feel as though that word is not strong enough for the fire that's ignited inside of me." My breath hitched as the space between us suddenly became warm from his body heat. I slid my hands up his shirt feeling every dip and crevice of his toned abdomen.

"Love is cruel. The feeling itself makes me feel full, yet when distance becomes a factor for whatever reason, love hurts with the intensity of a volcano. Like I said, I'm not experienced in this whole love department, but if I have to feel this type of whirlwind of an emotion, I choose to feel it for you."

My body is on fire now. His rawness is something I wasn't sure I would ever see. His darkness has always triumphed over anything light and airy, but this Dean right here could make a poet cry.

"I love you, baby girl."

I grabbed his face, pulling him to mine, and we kissed with the passion of a Shakespearean play. I wrapped my legs around his waist and debated never letting him go. If we had had more time, I'm sure I would have fucked him on this office desk, but the sound of someone's tongue clicking against their teeth had us stopping way too soon.

"Let's go, mate, the jet's waiting on us!" Colson yelled from the foyer.

"Please, be careful," I choked out.

"Always," Dean reassured me, and then the heat was suddenly ice cold as he joined the guys in the foyer. I followed him out of the office and watched as the guys each picked up their bags, tossing them over their shoulders and looking back at me one last time.

"The three of you come back to me. Alive." I crossed my arms and leaned against the doorframe to the office as the three men I loved walked out the door.

CHAPTER 26

DEAN

Reluctantly, the three of us boarded the jet that had been waiting for us at the airstrip. We each voiced our concerns with this arranged meeting and how our guts were all screaming for us not to go, but we quickly reminded ourselves this was for our girl. She deserves to meet the family she never knew existed. I just hoped they wanted to meet her as well.

The flight was relatively quick. We pulled on our serious faces and mentally prepared ourselves for whatever may happen. Although this meeting was mutually agreed upon, anyone that has connections with one of the biggest mobs this side of the world, had reason to be wary. My mindset going into this was trust no one—a motto I lived life by.

Trying to get my head in the game, I couldn't shake the image of Sloan's face as we left her at the castle. Concern etched across her beautiful face; my chest ached, leaving her like that. She loves me. She loves all of us, and we love her. Fuck. This meeting better be quick and smooth. I have a date with my girl that involves her in my bed for no less than twenty-four hours.

"Right, we are to meet with a gentleman named Kieran. He's been with The Wallace's since his father's passing six years ago. Sort of following in his father's footsteps, I suppose." Everett explained to us as he read through his laptop that was resting on his lap.

"Do we know his age?" I asked before he could continue.

He made a clicking noise with his tongue as he scrolled through his notes, trying to find the answer to my question.

"Ah, here we go; he's twenty-nine." He paused before continuing with his notes. "We are to meet Kieran at nine o'clock this evening at a private airstrip owned by the Wallace's, which is located in a town called Wicklow, South of Dublin. I've contacted a driver from our usual car service in the UK, who will be leaving a vehicle for us. We will then travel roughly twenty minutes to one of the Wallaces' estates, where we'll discuss business further." Everett paused and started rubbing the bridge of his nose in frustration.

"If that doesn't sound like the shadiest setup if I've ever heard one, mate. We've put too much control in their hands." Colson verbalized what we all had been thinking. "We couldn't have discussed business at the airstrip, so why must we travel into their territory?" Again, another valid question Colson brought to the table.

Closing his laptop, he let out a long sigh and then tossed back the last of his bourbon before answering. "This is not the most ideal meetup, I agree. I was informed that Mr. Kieran wouldn't be able to make it to the airstrip. I, too, suggested the meeting location be at the airstrip. His reasoning being, he's not comfortable discussing Mr. Wallace's family business in a public area. He prefers a private location. What I did manage to organize is four Shadows will be stationed around the location I provided, in case things go sour." Thank fuck, I thought to myself. I was not about to walk into something blind or without some sort of protection. I made a promise to my girl to come back alive, and I'll be damned if I break that promise.

There was a long silence in the room, the tension becoming a little less thick now that we knew we'd have backup of some sorts. The three of us soon became lost in our thoughts before Colson broke the silence.

"Did either of you two blokes ever think we'd all be in love with the same woman? An American woman at that?"

His question made me smirk, my lip turning up as I shook my head at him. "It's pretty fucking ironic, mate," I said, chuckling under my breath. I heard the huff of Everett beside me, he, too, letting slip a laugh at the revelation.

"She was destined for us, I suppose. We were meant to pick up that snatch-and-grab job. Imagine if we hadn't and she was sold off to one of those blood-thirsty monsters. No, mate, we were meant to kidnap her that day. If we hadn't, then we wouldn't have known she needed saving."

He was right. The unfortunate chain of events that led us to her ultimately had brought us together.

"How incredibly ironic," I muttered, tossing back my own glass of bourbon.

The pilot informed us we would be landing in the next thirty minutes. I glanced at my watch. That would mean wheels on the ground at six thirty in the evening.

"The four shadows are to arrive at the meeting location in the next fifteen minutes, and they will be positioning themselves around the property," Everett informed us as he scanned through his phone.

Perfect. The weight of this meeting started feeling a lot less heavy now that I knew we had our guys on the ground and in position, awaiting to intervene at a moment's notice. Let's hope it doesn't come to that.

As soon as we landed, the guys and I each grabbed our bags and started for the black SUV that sat at the corner of the airstrip. Everett settled in the driver's seat as I took up the passenger and Colson stretched out in the back. Colson then pulled out his laptop and began his coms with the four Shadows at the location. He was typing a mile a minute before he said, "Boys are in position and just informed me they've already counted eight men and one woman at the compound. The compound has two structures—one that's the main house by the looks of the size and the other a smaller building, all stone and off to the side of the compound near a narrow stream. Forest is dense near the stone building and well concealed. They say there's been a lot of movement in and out of the second building. No sign of Kieran just yet."

Everett started to drive away from the airstrip before responding, "I'm going to assume these pricks are going to use the smaller building as the meetup, but let's hope they don't try anything shady. I'm not against ending all their lives if they plan to fuck with us. I'm not in the mood right now."

Colson and I started strapping on our weapons, each of us having two secured in our chest holsters and a few blades discreetly hidden in our jeans and around our ankles. I also liked to carry my Glock 43X in my waistband, my go-to gun and the one I used most.

Along with preparing my own weapons, I started getting Everett's together for him as well. We never did anything without protection, and that's what kept us alive for this long. My only fear would be that they search us prior to entry, and if it came down to that, I doubt the meeting would go well at all. I never parted with my weapons. They were an extension of my own hands, never leaving my side.

The drive was quiet, the three of us dialed in and focused on the task at hand. It didn't take us long before we turned into a private gravel road that was full of twists and curves, leading us further and further into the forest.

"Right, Colson, go ahead and check with the guys once more. Tell them we are two mikes out and we're going ghost on coms, but to stay alert and listen for the call sign. They'll be able to hear us, but we won't hear them," Everett instructed while he slowed his speed as the road became more and more narrow and curvy.

"On it, mate," Colson said as he opened his laptop and went to work.

Pulling up to the location, I could see the main house off in the distance; however, the road we were currently on was taking us further into the woods. Like we'd guessed earlier, this would in fact be the location the meeting was going to be held at. As Everett followed the road, we drove through the circular path and stopped in front of two gentlemen that looked to be expecting us.

Reluctantly, the three of us exited the vehicle and approached the two men. We remained silent, waiting for them to make the first move or, rather, say the first words. One of the men put his hand in the air, indicating for us to stop, so we did.

"Arms to de side," the larger man told us with his thick Irish accent, and I knew he was about to search us. Fucking perfect. Neither of us moved. Everett stood at the head of our formation as Colson and I stood to his sides. Everett placed both of his hands in front of him, overlapping them as he tilted his head to the side.

"I don't believe that will be necessary. We're not here for trouble, so you can rest assured." Everett's tone was calm, not giving away any notion he was worried at all. The big man took a step forward, chest puffed out and a cock fight brewing between the five of us.

"It's standard prahcedure 'ere bahys. We know you're naht 'ere to cause any trooehble, but I moehst insest. It's de bahss man's pahlicy, I'm afraid." A husky voice and even stronger Irish accent came from behind the two men that grabbed our attention, as a hand clamped down on the two men's shoulders.

"We will not be following through with this meeting if we are the only ones unarmed. I take it you're Kieran," Everett said sternly. Kieran was a shorter man, possibly six feet, not short in normal standards but standing near the five other men that surrounded him, he was indeed the shortest. He was stocky, not fat, but carried a little more weight throughout his body. His hair was jet black and slicked back with way too much gel. He wore a shit-brown suit that did nothing for him, and a chain hung low from his side pocket to the back pocket. He was definitely the kind of guy that tried to act like a badass rather than actually being one.

"I can assure you; no one is going into dis buildin

armed. Dis'll be a peacefoehl meetin in regards to Mr. Wallace trackin down 'is grandkeds. 'E's been searchin fahr quite sahme time now," Kieran spoke again, his gravelly voice told me he was definitely a smoker. The three of us exchanged looks, Everett giving me a slight half wink, telling me to not give away all the weapons. Of course, I wasn't going to give up all the protection.

"Right, if we can see no one else is armed, we, too, will surrender our weapons. However, no need for one and two over there to get handsy and grab our dicks; we'll hand them over instead. Sound good, mate?"

There was a brief pause between Kieran and the two other guys, but they soon all nodded and the three of us got to work unstrapping our weapons one at a time. We each had another Glock strapped to the midsection of our backs, fastened so it was positioned with the handle down for easy retrieval. This was the gun we'd all keep strapped to us. Most people when they are being searched are asked to raise their shirts to prove nothing is hidden in the waistband, but almost always people never assume there is a gun strapped to the spine of their opponent's back.

Going through the ensemble of weaponry we each had hidden on ourselves, I discreetly looked around the property and saw some motion cameras at the points of the building, some located on trees, and a few in the driveway pointed towards the vehicles.

Apart from the three blokes in front of us, I saw no other people around the compound.

"Your turn, Kieran," I said, standing up tall and giving him a look of death. He turned and gave me a pointed look, and then a small smile curled up with lips not reaching his eyes.

"Since myself and my two guards will be the only ones in attendance, you can see we, too, have no weapons on us." He raised his suit jacket first and spun around, allowing us to see his back and no weapons in his waistband. The two guards did the same, each pulling out what looked to be Smith and Wesson handguns and placing them on the floor along with our weapons.

As soon as we all established we weren't armed, except the three of us now, Kieran waved his hand and ushered us to follow him as we made our way to the path leading to the stone building. As uneasy as I was that I only had one gun strapped to my back, I was also glad we had eight eyes on us, rifles at the ready, in case shit hit the fan. Kieran opened the door and stepped through first while the two guards who stood on either side of the door waited for the three of us to enter behind him.

Again, we hesitated, Everett looking over his shoulder at the two of us, giving us a small nod and stepped over the threshold of the door. Following close behind, Colson and I stepped through the door and an immediate chill sank into my bones.

The room was dark, the only source of light being

two overhead lights that dimly lit the room. In the center of the room was a rectangular table with a few chairs neatly placed underneath. Besides the table and chairs, the room was completely empty. There were no windows or other doors leading out of the building. My gut turned with dread and concern about the outcome of this meeting.

The three of us as soon as we entered the room immediately turned our bodies so our backs were no longer facing the door. Kieran and the two guards came into the room and immediately found a place at the table. Kieran sat in the chair facing the door, while the two guards stood directly behind him. That left the chairs with the backs towards the door for us to take. That wasn't happening.

"Please, gentleman, take a seat," Kieran insisted as he waved his hand to the table. Everett looked between Colson and I, giving us a slight nod. He then took a seat while the both of us stood off to the side, giving us a full view of the room around us. We weren't fucking stupid; we would never leave ourselves vulnerable like that. Kieran chuckled and shook his head as he watched the three of us take up our positions. Bastard.

"Gentleman, we are all 'ere to descoehss de family matters o' Mr. Wallace trackin' down 'is lahst grandcheld. Am I right?" he asked, pulling out a cigarette and lighting the end while taking a deep inhale. Without addressing him verbally, Everett nodded his head once and awaited a response from Kieran.

"Well den, Sloan, is it?" Kieran gestured to Everett with his hand that held the cigarette firmly between his fingers. "Sloan is one o' three grandcheldren to Mr. Wallace. De twins Cara and Cormac were bot so oehnfartunate enooehgh to 'ave lahst deir mahther durin deir birth. Dey grew oehp wit deir mahternall grandmahther, Cecil, oehntil 'er oehntimely deat, in whech Mr. Wallace took dem in." He paused a moment, taking more deep inhales of his cigarette before he continued. "Now, I'm tahld you are wantin to set oehp a meetin with de twens?" Kieran looked between the three of us. It was Everett who answered.

"Kieran, before I answer that, may I ask you a question first?"

Kieran nodded once and tilted his head to the side in confusion. "How long have you been with the Wallace family? I hear your father worked for him prior to his death. There was a long pause where Kieran just stared at Everett, showing no emotion.

"Me father and I 'ave been wit Mr. Wallace sence befahre I was bahrn. Ooer families are clahse and derefarhe it was always in me future to fahllow me father's footsteps and serve dis family."

Everett adjusted himself in his chair, spreading his legs wide and settling in. "You see, Kieran, our girl has never had a family, and when we found out about the twins, you can imagine her excitement to have blood relatives she could possibly bond with. With that said, we are aware that Mr. Wallace is currently not in the best of health. We need to ensure the twins have all the right intentions before Sloan is brought in."

The smile that curled up Kieran's face had the hairs on the back of my neck standing straight up. "You see, mates, when it combs to Mr. Wallace's 'ealth is indeed declinin rapedly, and soon 'e'll will soehc-coehmb to 'is illness. Whech den begs de question, who is to take over dis empire, so to speak." Kieran then pulled out from beneath the table what looked to be a mask as did the two guards. "I've been lahyal to Mr. Wallace me whahle life, and I know 'ow truly 'appy 'e'll be when 'e knows Sloan is alive and 'e'll soon be able to meet 'er. Dat is o' cooehrse, 'e does naht die first."

Just then the three men pulled the masks over their faces as a thick billow of smoke started pouring from a few vents hidden within the rocks of the walls that I hadn't noticed before. Instantly my throat began to feel restricted as the thick plume of gas started to quickly suffocate Colson, Everett and me. The room was soon engulfed in a cloud of smoke, and my vision started to darken. Looking over, I saw Colson had already collapsed against the wall, since he was standing directly beside one of the vents. Everett was kneeling on the ground, clenching his throat as he struggled to breathe.

I started to stumble my way to Everett, but the sound of the heavy wooden door opening caught my attention. Falling to the floor beside Everett, I tried squinting to see who now stood in the room. Two dark figures, each wearing masks, stood over Everett and myself before saying, "Too bad Sloan wasn't 'ere. Dis wooehld 'ave been too easy." A female voice filled the room just as my head hit the floor and the dark tunnel of unconsciousness blanketed my vision. What the fuck is happening?

CHAPTER 27

SLOAN

It's been seventy-two hours. Twenty-four hours longer than they said they would be. Something isn't right, something is wrong. They haven't contacted Cain or Stone, and I could feel the tension and concern whenever I entered a room they were in.

Pacing the kitchen, I was picking at my nails, a nervous habit I'd done since forever. It wasn't until I felt the light stream of blood sliding down my hand that I noticed I had picked the skin so badly around my cuticle that I was now bleeding. Fuck.

"Why haven't they called yet? I asked Cain as he sat at the island typing away at his laptop.

"I'm trying to find you an answer," he responded, sounding equally as concerned but also annoyed that I'd asked this question roughly six times already.

"Something's wrong. I can feel it," I murmured out loud, not talking to anyone in particular but mainly just thinking aloud. As I continued to pace the room, the sound of the front door startled me, and I took off to see who it was.

Stone stormed through the door, his heavy boots stomping through the foyer as he headed to the kitchen with his phone clenched in his hand. Entering the kitchen, he slammed his phone on the granite countertop, no doubt shattering his screen, and said to Cain, "They've been taken. All three of them. One of the Shadows outside the complex said they entered the stone building but have yet to exit. Many people have been seen going in and out, including a female. They've said with the resources they have guarding the building, it's not wise for the four of them to infiltrate the building without getting eyes inside first."

My breath hitched, and a sharp pain stabbed through my chest making its way down to the pit of my stomach.

"We do know they're alive. Everett has his mic still turned on, so the Shadows are able to hear everything that's happening inside." Stone's face fell as he turned to look at me before continuing. "You may want to give us a minute alone, Sloan."

As the feeling of dread bubbled inside me, another feeling also started to ignite as his words circled my brain. "The fuck if I'm leaving. Whatever it is you're about to say, you can say it in front of me." My voice was pure venom as rage started to turn my blood from red to black. I'd never felt this type of anger before. It felt like my skin was on fire as every one of my muscles flexed against my skin. He didn't respond right away. He just kept looking at me as if I was going to back down and leave the room. My composure snapped then, "Fucking say what you have to say, Stone!"

He flinched at my sudden outburst, but I didn't care. My guys were taken, and I needed to know what the hell was going on. He finally sighed, turning to Cain who gave him a nod of approval to continue.

"It seems as though Everett, Dean, and Colson are being tortured in order to give up Sloan's location. They've reported hearing whips, power tools, chains, water, and more sounds they're not able to pinpoint the source of. They haven't said a word, the three of them. Just sounds of them grunting, moaning, and screaming have been heard but they haven't broken. Not yet, anyway."

They're being tortured? My skin started to tingle, and I could hear the grinding of my teeth as I clenched my jaw so hard, I thought I might break a tooth. They went to Ireland for me, to try and build a family bond with people I've never met. They knew how important family was to me, so they were willing to put themselves at risk to try and give me something I've only ever dreamt of. I've been wishing and praying for a family that loves me and truly cares for me in the deepest of ways. But I never had to look any further than what was in my face all along.

I didn't need blood to determine family. Everett, Colson, and Dean have shown me more love and more passion than anyone in this world could possibly show me. Yet I was blind to the simple word, family. I never thought that some families don't share blood. How could I've let this happen? How could I've been so blind that I allowed them to travel to unfamiliar territories to meet the fucking Irish mob in hopes of finding who? My dearest grandfather? Yeah, fucking right, if they were family, they wouldn't have let me live this life for so long. They weren't family. Right now, they were my enemy.

"How did you find this information?" My voice was calm as I asked both Cain and Stone. This was no time for tears. I needed to find a way to my guys. They've saved me an endless number of times; it's my turn.

"Our Shadows' contact," Stone replied.

Before he could say a name, I asked firmly, "What Shadow? Who is it, and how can I get a hold of them?"

The two of them just stared at me as if they just saw a ghost.

"Tell me now," I said again, all signs of the old Sloan out the window. This new Sloan that I didn't recognize had taken over me, and she was no bitch to fuck with.

"Uhm, well listen, Sloan," Cain said, closing his laptop, but I cut him off.

"Tell me who the fuck I need to talk to in order to get my guys back! Who gave you the information, Stone?" I screamed a demonic sound as I spat my words at the two of them. They quickly got the hint and Stone replied, "Arno. He's been tasked with this op as well, and he's currently the one feeding us the intel on the guys."

That was not who I was expecting.

"Arno! You've got to be joking?" I rolled my eyes as I lowered my head in frustration. "Give me your phone, Stone. Pull up his number and give it to me."

He looked at Cain, utter shock plastered across his face.

"Don't look at him. I told you what I needed. Now give me the fucking phone. Now! The longer you play stupid, the more our guys get hurt. Now give me the fucking phone."

He did as I said, no longer looking to Cain for confirmation.

"It's ringing," Stone said to me as he handed over the phone. Two rings traveled through my ear before I heard his voice.

"I told you I'd call when I had more information." Arno's voice came through the phone, and I couldn't believe what I was about to say.

"Arno, it's me, Sloan. I need your help." There was a long pause. I could only imagine the look on his face, hearing my voice instead of Stone's.

"And what could I possibly do for you, little one?"

I rolled my eyes at his nickname, but knowing he was Shadows as well, he had the resources I needed to save my guys.

"I need you to get me to Ireland as quickly as possible."

He responded almost instantly. "What do you think you're going to—"

I cut him off, "I plan on paying my grandfather a visit and showing him just exactly who I am while getting my guys back. I take it you have the skills to help out, since you, too, are a part of the Shadows? Or do I need to find someone more qualified?" Scoffing into the receiver, I could hear him talking to someone but couldn't make out what he was saying.

A second later, he said, "Sloan, get a bag together. Give the phone to Stone and have him take you to the nearest airstrip. Have him give me the coordinates to that location, and we will be there to pick you up." Sighing into the phone, he continued, "I hope you know what you're getting yourself into, little one."

"Just get here," I said before sliding the phone across the granite island to Stone.

I left the kitchen to head to my room and pack a bag as he instructed, but just as I was leaving the kitchen, I heard Cain say to Stone, "The guys are going to kill us, mate."

I chuckled because, yeah, maybe they would, but right now all I was focused on was getting them back and killing whoever had put hands on them.

Arno was at the airstrip waiting for us, along with Jei and Stefan. Stone and Cain had reluctantly done everything I told them too. After ending the call with Arno, they did everything they could to try and convince me to stay put and let the Shadows handle rescuing the guys, but I wasn't having any of it.

Pulling up to the airstrip, a small jet sat ready as I grabbed my bag and exited the SUV. Stone and Cain followed behind me as we made our way to the jet where the guys were waiting.

"You do know we're all dead if anything happens to her, right?" Arno addressed Cain and Stone, looking over the top of my head.

"Yeah, we get that, but what the fuck do you want us to do, mate? Everett said we couldn't lay a hand on her, so tying her up was out of the question," Cain barked right back.

"Nothing is going to happen to me. Stop whining and get in the jet. We need to leave now before anything else happens to them." I pushed past Arno, stomping up the stairs to the jet. Jei, Stefan, Arno, Cain, and Stone all followed behind me, each one taking up a seat except for Jei. He made his way to the cockpit, strapping himself in. These men really did know how to do everything. Arno took the seat in front of me, fastening his seatbelt and leaning on his elbows on his thick thighs.

"Listen, Sloan, this might get bloody. I can't have you and your emotions getting in the way and getting yourself or someone else killed." His tone was stern but also empathetic. This was a side of Arno I never thought I'd see. "You need to listen to everything I tell you to do. I have a plan, but—"

I cut him off again, "I understand, Arno. Don't be

a bitch. Don't let my emotions take over. Follow your rules. I get it, okay? Now what's the plan?

He looked down at the floor, shaking his head, but when he looked back up, his eyes had completely changed. His whole demeanor had changed from cocky, arrogant, douchebag to stone-faced, all-business mercenary. His eyes turned dark as oil. He cracked his neck and clapped his hands together once.

"Okay, we still have four guys on the ground, but they haven't been able to get into the building due to high security. We have an assortment of weapons with us that will allow us to eliminate these targets quietly so we can gain access to where they are being held." He paused as the jet took off, waiting for the jet to level out before continuing. "Once we're in, there is no telling what state we're going to find them in. We've been hearing all sorts of things, Sloan, and none of them are good. This is when you need to keep your composure locked in tight. It won't be easy to see, but this is what I need from you to ensure we all get home alive. Understood?"

I nodded, not really knowing what to say to him. My stomach was clenching so hard as the butterflies in my gut started raging war on each other. I've never feared losing someone before. I've never loved anyone enough to truly care about their well-being. Yet sitting here now, I can't imagine losing my three guys; it would be like losing a piece of my heart.

I was fidgeting in my chair and staring out the

window when a loud chiming noise startled me out of my thoughts. Thank fuck, really, because I was starting to imagine the worst-case scenarios, which made my whole body ridged. Looking up at Arno, I saw he was opening his laptop, which he had stored in his bag below his feet.

"One of the guys activated their cameras. Each one of the guys on the ground have a camera mounted on their vest," Arno informed me as he started clicking through his security blocks and finally accepted the video. "They won't be able to hear us, but we will be able to see what they are seeing. Evidently, it's important enough to videotape and record. This is the first video we've received." He squinted at his laptop before saying, "It looks as though he's detached his camera and fitted it between a few stones." There was a long pause. Then Arno rubbed his hand down his face. "Fucking hell." I immediately jumped out of my chair to sit next to Arno and see what he was seeing. Before I could see anything, though, Arno quickly spun the laptop away from my view.

"What the fuck, Arno, let me see. Now!" I hollered at him as I tried to reach for his laptop, which he was now lifting above his head away from me.

"Sloan, stop it! For fuck's sake. It's not good. They wouldn't want you to see this!" he yelled back before I elbowed him so swiftly in his gut, he hunched over enough that I was able to grab his laptop and bring it to my lap. What I saw I was truly and utterly not prepared for.

All three of my guys hung from the ceiling, their arms tied above their heads and their feet barely able to touch the floor. Blood trickled down all of their wrists, the strain of the ropes cutting into their skin. This wasn't even the worst part. Each one of them had their shirts removed, and crimson blood coated their chests from what looked to be long slashing wounds, maybe from a whip? Colson's left eye was so swollen that it was completely shut, and his hair was no longer golden blond, but darkish brown and red from dried blood.

Dean's nose was sitting in an awkward position, almost a zigzag shape across his battered face. His rib cage now displayed a long rectangular wound that was glistening with bright red blood, but this blood was not dripping down his body, rather it was oozing as if the wound was deep enough to tear skin, but not deep enough to produce large amounts of blood.

"That looks to be from a medical device that removes portions of skin for skin grafts. Sort of like a cheese slicer, if you will," he said, pointing at Dean's wound as though he was seeing the confusion on my face. I covered my mouth in sheer horror while the sting of tears started to form in the backs of my eyes.

Everett was swinging in the middle, between the two, and his wounds looked to be the worst. He was covered in blood, so much blood. I couldn't even make out his wounds. His whole body looked like he was dipped in red paint. His beautiful face was lifted to the ceiling in defiance, while whoever was in the room with them was talking to him specifically.

I couldn't make out what was being said and neither could Arno. But then he was able to increase the volume on the camera enough so that we could hear what was being said.

"Now, I 'ave to admit, you three are strahng mahther foockers. Anyone else wooehld 'ave given oehp 'er lahcation by now, but you goeys." The female talking was waving her finger at the three of my guys. Rage started to boil inside me once again, and all I wanted to do was snap her delicate little finger in two. "You've known 'er fahr less dan a year, and she is wahrthy 'o dis type 'o prahtection. Well, shet bahys, she moehst be a damn good foock if you're stell gaoehrdin 'er."

Dean struggled against his restraints and was about to say something until a loud crackling noise broke across the room followed by a deep growl from Dean. Someone else was in the room, and they had just whipped Dean's back, causing blood to spray through the air.

I flinched as the sound pierced my ears.

"Fucking hell, mate," Arno said in a low voice beside me. He looked equally as horrified, staring at my guys, but no doubt he'd seen this type of torture before. Especially in his line of work.

"Joehst tell me de lahcation, and all dis pain'll go away," the woman said again as she spread her arms to the side, mocking the guy's current position. There wasn't a sound from either of the three; they just hung there from their ropes continuing to protect me. I started to shake as the fear and rage filtered throughout my body. My knee started to bounce, causing the laptop to jiggle in my lap.

"Let me hold this, Sloan. We need to be able to see everything inside that building. It'll help us when we go in." He took the laptop from me, but my eyes followed, never leaving the screen.

I felt a stray tear creep down my cheek, but I quickly brushed it away, not wanting anyone to see my emotions. My eyes combed over each one of them. Colson hung to Everett's left, his chest rising and falling in short shallow breaths as though he was trying to calm his body. Dean was hanging to Everett's right. His eyes trained on the woman standing before them. His stare promised a very, very painful death once he was free. Then there was Everett, his expression almost annoyed and unbothered by their situation. Everett had a talent for not giving away his emotions, he was an iron clasp that never broke. If he was in pain, and I had no doubt he was, he never showed the slightest bit of pain, even though his body was currently dripping blood from numerous wounds all across his body.

"They need to get in there now and save them, Arno. Why haven't they moved in yet?" I started to feel desperate, my fear of losing them beginning to build to unmanageable levels. Arno reached for my hand, but I quickly snatched it away before he could touch me.

"Sloan, again, you can't let your feelings for them get in the way. There are only four guys on the ground now and what seems to be a dozen, if not more, highly armed men surrounding the building they're being held in. That's not even counting the people in the main house. We have to be smart about this. Plus, I've told them to stand down until we arrive with their backup."

Before I could stop myself, I slapped Arno so hard across the face, his head fell to the side. He didn't flinch, though. He just cracked his neck and looked back up at me, fire blazing in his eyes.

"I suggest you take your seat, firecracker, or I will sit you down myself."

I held his gaze, both of us staring daggers at one another before a heavy hand clamped down on my shoulder, breaking my focus.

"Sit down, Sloan. We need everyone's head in the game for this one," Cain said to me as he raised an eyebrow and looked between Arno and me. As if they were having a telepathic conversation, Arno directed his gaze back to the laptop while I took my seat again and turned to his laptop once again.

"I 'aven't gaht de time fahr dis shet anymahre. Either you tell me where she is, ahr I'll start eliminatin each o' you oehntil sahmeone speaks oehp."

My heart sank as the woman pulled out a Glock 47

from her waistband and pointed it between the three of them.

"No, no, no, no, no. Please!" I screamed at the screen as if she could hear me. I took the laptop from Arno's hands and pulled it close to my chest as my eyes followed the gun she was pointing.

"Loehcky betch doesn't need all three 'o you. 'Ow selfesh can a wahman get?"

Her chuckle had me biting the inside of my cheek. I silently promised myself I was going to kill this woman, whoever she was.

"Nothing you say or do will ever get us to tell you anything, Cara. I suggest you move on with whatever you think you have planned for us, because, frankly, I'm getting quite bored of this. Dontcha think, boys?" Everett glanced down at the dirt-covered floor, but I didn't miss the slight smile he gave the camera before quickly looking back up to the woman.

"He sees the camera, smart bastard," Arno said aloud with a chuckle.

"Naht smart, temptin' de persahn who's gaht you tied oehp. Oehnless you're naht scared or merely dink I'm all talk and wahn't end one o you right now." The woman we now knew as Cara spat out while she got right in Everett's face. Cara and Everett both held each other's gazes until the crack of a bullet pierced through the air.

CHAPTER 28

SLOAN

The scream that escaped from me sounded almost demonic as I clutched the sides of Arno's laptop so hard, I could feel the cracking of the screen beneath my fingers. My eyes were scouring through the pixelated image as I tried to make out the chaos that was unfolding. Glancing through each of my guys, my eyes landed on Colson, his now lifeless body hanging by the ropes as blood pooled from a fresh wound in his lower abdomen.

"Colson! Nooo!" I cried out as tears started cascading down my cheeks uncontrollably. "No, please, no!" I was shaking the laptop as if I were shaking Colson. My stomach felt as though someone had just stabbed me with a butcher's knife and started twisting it around.

"No, no, no, this isn't happening! This can't happen!" I couldn't look away from the horror in front of me. Colson, the man who held a third of my heart, head slumped towards the ground as his body swung back and forth from the bullet's impact. There was no sound coming from the video. Everett and Dean maintained their composure as if Colson being shot meant nothing to them. However, I knew the war that was now raging inside both of them as their brother hung unconscious.

Dean's chest rose and fell with deep breaths as he tried to hold in his inner demon that would soon break free. Everett's face was utterly still; he never even flinched as the gunshot pierced the air. Just then Colson's body hit the floor with a loud thump, as a man behind him cut the rope that was suspending him in the air. The sound of his body hitting the dirt had me gasping. His body remained still.

"Please, someone help them, please!" I turned to Arno as I cried out, my voice cracking with every word. "Arno, please, please, do something." I was shattering from the inside out, my chest felt like a forest fire, blazing so hot the pain was unbearable. Looking from Arno to the computer, I saw the camera flicker as the feed suddenly went black.

"No, no, no! What's happening? Come back! Where'd they go?" I was shaking the laptop now until it was suddenly ripped from my grasp and a strong pair of arms surrounded me in an embrace. Arno had grabbed me and pulled me close to his chest as I sobbed uncontrollably into his large frame. My knees buckled, and I slid to the ground of the jet, but Arno held me, lowering me slowly as he maintained his embrace.

I'm not sure how long I was crying for. All I know is when I came to, I was sitting in Arno's lap, his strong arms holding me tight as he allowed me to crumble. Just then, Jei turned around from the cockpit and told us we were five minutes out from the landing strip and that we needed to get in our seats. I felt so heavy, my skin burned with rage. I made no effort to move from where I was.

Arno lifted me as if I weighed nothing and sat me back in my seat before proceeding to buckle me in. He then took the seat beside me and began strapping himself in as well. There was a long silence in the small jet before Arno's voice broke the silence.

"Sloan, look at me." I did as he said and looked up at him. "We'll get them back, I promise."

I believed him. This was not the Arno I was used to. I'm not sure when my feelings for Arno changed, but the fact that he was here helping me try and get my guys back spoke volumes. Not to mention he just spent however long on the floor of this plane holding and comforting me as I slowly started to die myself.

"Snap out of it, Sloan, we don't know if he's dead or just hurt. Get your shit together and get your head in the game. Remember what I told you. Leave your emotions at the door; we need to get them home alive." Arno was right. I needed to stop assuming the worst and pull myself together. I would be of no help if I remained a sobbing mess. Wiping my eyes of tears, I straightened my back and began taking long, deep breaths.

"Good, now let's go fuck some Irish pricks up." Arno put his fist in front of mine. Looking at him for a moment, I nodded once in agreement and bumped his fist with mine.

"That's it, little one, welcome to the Shadows." With those words the plane touched to the ground with a thud, and it was go time.

I obviously had no training when it came to mercenary shit—I mean, who really did besides like one percent of people? So, when Arno handed me a gun, I looked up at him with a childlike expression.

"I've never used a gun before," I admitted. He just let out a small chuckle as he began strapping guns all over his body, some concealed, some visible.

"Just point and shoot. Just, don't shoot me," Arno winked at me. Who the fuck was this man? This was a far jump from the Arno I'd met back at Stone Fortress. It made me wonder if the arrogant douchebag facade was just that, a facade. Was it all an act to try and seem tough? Concealing the gun in the waistband of my jeans, I started to wonder if I could in fact fully trust Arno.

Cain and Stone exited the jet first, as Jei, Arno, Stefan, and me followed behind. Stepping off the jet, I saw the sky was dark and the air felt crisp. The wind was strong as it cut through the sweatshirt I was wearing, and I flinched at the sudden chill. We were at a very, and I mean very, small airstrip. In fact, it looked as though it was just a clear-cut field with grass beneath my feet. There was nothing around us but forest, until a pair of headlights I hadn't seen at first emerged from a road.

"Right, here's our ride. We'll be taken to the outskirts of the property, roughly ten minutes away. Once we get there, we have a mile trek through the forest that lines the back of the compound. We'll then meet up with the four Shadows on the ground and strategize our entry point." Arno addressed the lot of us, but then turned to face me. "Sloan, remember what I told you, emotions are turned off from this moment on. You need to be on alert, everyone is an enemy to you. Trust no one." I kept my face hard as I nodded my understanding, but I would be lying if I said I wasn't scared shitless.

We all climbed into the blacked-out Suburban. I crawled into the back to the third row, and Jei followed close behind. Arno took up the front passenger seat as Cain, Stone, and Stefan sat in the middle row. The driver was oddly familiar to me. I just couldn't pinpoint where I'd seen him before. The man was fairly large, his broad shoulders were wider than the driver's seat he was currently sitting in. A dragon tattoo snaked up his neck from beneath his long sleeve shirt he was wearing. I studied him for a while as the guys situated themselves, adjusting their weapons so they could sit more comfortably in the now packed vehicle.

"Where are the others going to sit?" I asked Jei,

keeping my voice low. But it wasn't Jei who answered me.

"We have another vehicle already in place, brought to the location by our four Shadows on the ground," Arno answered, not turning his head to face me as he spoke.

We made our way down a dirt road that was pitch-black except for the headlights from our vehicle. This road was curvy and eerie, the kind of road you would see in a horror film. The irony of that, though, had my stomach turning. We were in fact starring in our own horror film. The friend's crew is racing to save the characters who've been captured, and let's just hope there's a happy ending with this flick.

Staring out the window, I started to see a very dim light shining through the trees up ahead. My palms started to sweat as flashes of the video danced across my vision. The vision of Colson's lifeless form lying on the cold, mucky ground had my chest tightening, and I could feel the threat of tears stinging the back of my eyes. Remembering what Arno said, I quickly shook my head and blinked away the sight, pushing away the emotions building within.

"Two minutes out," the driver announced, and I peered through the windshield as the lights shined brighter as we approached. Squinting, I could make out another vehicle pointing its headlights toward us, which blinded me from seeing anything else. Our vehicle came to a stop as the shadow of two men moved in front of the headlights.

"Let's be quick; time is of the essence," Arno said, opening his door and stepping out. The rest of us followed, with Jei and me the last to exit the vehicle.

"Right, we haven't been able to get cameras inside the building since our last transmission. We have also yet to see anyone leave the building since the incident, which means all the key players are still inside." One of the Shadows addressed Arno as we all listened intently. "I'll need two of you to hang back here to watch the vehicles and be ready. I imagine this is going to be a hot extraction." There was a pause as the man looked at me and then back to Arno. "I suggest she stay behind as well."

Before I could open my mouth in protest Arno spoke. "She comes with us."

The man rolled his eyes, obviously annoyed.

"I can't promise her safety with this extraction, mate. I suggest—" He was cut off before he could finish.

"She's coming. She knows the risk, and I'll ensure she gets out alive." Arno looked at me over his shoulder, giving me a hard look as if waiting for me to agree. I nodded once, keeping my face neutral and equally as hard.

"Right, your funeral, mate. Everett won't like this." The man shook his head and pinched the bridge of his nose before continuing. "We have a mile hike to the holding place. Once we get there, we have two more men who will give you details on the building. Then we'll breach the building, extract the hostages, and move out. Clear?" We all nodded our heads. "Let's hope this goes smoothly. I'm over this fucking place already, and I'm in dire need of a shower." With that we all began our trek through the forest, while Cain and Stone remained with the vehicles.

The two Shadows led the way, with Arno and me following close behind. Bringing up the rear was Jei and Stefan, and in my position, I felt surprisingly safe. I was in fact with six Shadow members, the organization who dealt with raising, training, and molding these men into ruthless mercenaries. How much safer could a girl be?

"You are to stay right beside me, little one. No wandering off; you remain by my side until we reach the vehicles again. Understood?" Arno's voice was stern, and for a split second I imagined this was how an older brother would sound protecting his younger sister.

"Understood," I whispered back to him as I subconsciously stepped a little closer to him while we continued walking.

Normally, a mile feels like it takes ages to end; however, this mile was by far the quickest mile I'd ever walked. My insides felt as though someone was twisting my organs in a knot, my mouth was drier than the Sahara Desert, and my head was swimming with every possible outcome this situation could have. But above all else my heart was aching from the thought of losing any one of my guys. This was my opportunity to repay them for all the times they'd saved me. I could be the one to save their lives and bring them all home so we could continue to live this crazy polyamorous relationship we've created together. I could be their hero for once, like they've become mine.

I inhaled a deep breath and pinched my eyes shut hard. When I opened them, I was no longer the scared, timid, and the weak little girl they'd saved from Stone Fortress. I was Sloan reborn. No longer would I allow fear to hold me back. I would embrace the darkness, walk into the abyss of dread, and welcome it with open arms. Suddenly, I felt nothing. As though the simple act of closing my eyes erased any, and all, sensations my body was once feeling only two minutes ago. I felt nothing. I was totally and completely numb. The only thought going through my mind was to get the guys, kill whoever stood in our way, and leave. I had a mission, and I was going to complete it.

"Are you okay, Sloan?" Arno's voice snapped me out of the trance I was in. I hadn't realized he had stopped walking and was now standing right in front of me. Looking up into his face, I saw his brows were furrowed and he looked utterly confused as he peered down at me.

"I'm fine; let's do this. In and out, we all get home alive." I pushed past Arno but was quickly stopped by a strong hand grabbing my upper arm. I was jerked back by Arno, our bodies colliding as he pulled me in close to him.

"What are you doing?" I protested, pressing my hands to his hard chest but not being able to move out of his grasp. His hands held me tight to his frame, his dark eyes peering down at me. He didn't respond right away; he just stared down at me as though he wanted to say something but ultimately chose not to.

"Just remember what I told you." Releasing my arms, he started walking again but not before he grabbed my hand and pulled me close behind him. We walked a little bit further like this, hand in hand, and I immediately felt that Arno cared for me. Not in the way Everett, Dean, and Colson did, but he did care for me. Why? I wasn't sure. I left Stone Fortress thinking he hated me with every inch of his being, but at this moment, hand in hand, I knew he truly cared for me. Whatever, I wasn't focused on the feelings Arno may or may not have for me. I was focused on my mission. Getting my guys back.

CHAPTER 29

SLOAN

We approached two of the remaining Shadows that had been tasked with watching over the compound, and we all gathered in a tight huddle to discuss the plan. We didn't waste time with introductions. I listened intently as the men went into grave detail about the building the guys were being held captive in. They explained the building was small, roughly 14x14 feet with no windows and one door leading in and out. They informed us that besides our three men, there are four other people inside currently—one being the female who shot Colson. Two men who looked to be guards for the woman, and another gentleman they claim to be the woman's second in command.

"We've yet to learn the name of Cara's second, but the other two men inside are merely guards. The grunt workers, if you will. Besides the four of them, no one else has been seen going in or out." The Shadow pulled out a small folded up piece of paper and started carefully unfolding it. It looked to be a hand drawn map of the compound. There was the main building as well as small walkways that led to either the front of the house or to the building where my guys were being held. There was also a small building, a shed maybe, on the far end of the property, secluded from any other buildings on the property.

"What is this?" I asked, pointing to the shed on the map. The man looked up from the map and gave me a double take before answering.

"That's their security building. It looks to always be occupied by one man. We've infiltrated their system and will be running a looped segment of footage while we're taking the building." I looked to Arno who was nodding his head in approval. The Shadow holding the map gave me another curious look, which Arno noticed as well.

"She's coming with us, mate, so I suggest holding your tongue with whatever you're about to say." Arno's voice was ice cold, a tremor of possessiveness rippling through his posture as he inches a little bit closer to me. The other Shadow says nothing, just dips his head in understanding before we continue going over the plan. We're instructed that we will breach the door with a mini explosive that will stick to the hinges of the door frame and once we gain entry, Arno and the two Shadows will sweep the room before Stefan, Jei, and me reach the guys and begin freeing their restraints.

The guys draw their weapons, and Arno gives me a look over his broad shoulder. I do the same with the Glock he gave me. We all get in position, and I'm standing right behind Arno as we start moving quickly and quietly through the woodland area we've been hiding in and make our way around the building. My heart is pounding, and I fear the guys can hear the loud thumping as I feel it beating against my chest.

Reaching the door, the two Shadows place the explosive devices on the two hinges and step away. We all take a step back, and the guys give a nod to gesture we're all ready. I close my eyes hard and take a deep breath in. *You can do this, Sloan, you're strong; they need you.*

The blast of the explosives reverberates throughout my body, and my ears ring just slightly as everyone begins to move. Arno disappears into the building, and I follow a few steps behind, allowing them to clear the room. Walking over the threshold, I can feel my heart, which seems like it quite literally is cracking in half at the sight of my guys.

"Clear," someone says.

"Clear," another voice says.

"Where the fuck are the Irishmen?" Arno's voice asks, but I can't focus on anything other than my guys. Everett and Dean are both hanging from their restraints. Both unconscious, blood dripping from all over their bodies. Their wounds are so extensive I can't see even an inch of their skin that isn't drenched with fresh or dried blood. They're alive, though. The slow rise and fall of their chests tells me they're still here. Then my eyes fall to the floor. My body feels like a magnet as I rush to Colson's lifeless body lying in a pool of his blood.

"Colson! Colson, please wake up! Can you hear me?" I turn his body over, and I gasp. His torso is drenched in blood, which is oozing out of his gunshot wound in his abdomen.

"Fuck! Please, Colson, open your eyes for me." I can hear the guys behind me working on getting Everett and Dean freed from their restraints, but my world is closing in on me as I fear we're too late.

"Wake up! Please, baby, wake up!" My hands are shaking as I cup Colson's face. His beautiful face is covered in dried blood, and his hair is sticking to the side of his face he was lying on. I can feel the slightest beat of a pulse on his neck, but his breathing is so shallow I feel I might be imagining it. I can feel someone kneel beside me and a heavy hand landing on my shoulder.

"Sloan, we have to go. I've got him. Go with Jei. We need to get to the car before someone comes to investigate the explosion," Arno instructs. I couldn't pull my eyes away from Colson's body. His once vibrant soul and golden tanned skin looks ashen and frail as Arno lifts his limp frame over his large shoulders. His head bobs off his back, and a sob escapes me. Jei pulls me from the floor and grabs my hand in his.

"Sloan, emotions get you killed. Remember what Arno told you?"

Jei was right. I couldn't get emotional now; we needed to get out and fast. The other two Shadows had Everett and Dean slumped over their own shoulders in a fireman's carry. Stefan waited for Jei and me to exit the building before following close behind.

"Where were the others that were supposed to be in the building?" I asked Jei as we all started rushing to the wood line and back to our waiting vehicle.

"There was a trapped door in the corner; it looked to be their way in and out without being seen." I looked over my shoulder to see if anyone was following us, but there was no one. We continued running, and I couldn't shake the feeling that something was wrong. It had been too easy. I expected utter chaos once we entered the building, but there was nothing. Just my guys. Where were the guards and the woman?

Reaching our vehicle, I let out a breath and internally smiled as the finish line was approaching. We did it. We got our guys and now to get them medical attention and fast. Just as we approached the vehicle, I was suddenly thrown from my feet. Our vehicle was suddenly completely engulfed in flames as our getaway car exploded into a giant fireball. Fuck!

Landing flat on my back, I try to catch my breath

as the wind is knocked clear out of my lungs. Coughing and gasping for air, my body is quickly lifted from the ground as Jei picks me up as though I weigh absolutely nothing to him. He quickly scans my body looking for injuries, but to my surprise I'm relatively unscathed. Just a few scratches on my back start to sting from being thrown to the forest floor.

"You all right?" Jei asks me in a hurried voice. I cough a few times but nod my head up and down. Looking around, I see our crew have already found their bearings and have picked up Everett, Dean, and Colson since they are still all unconscious.

"We need to get out of here and make our way to point B for extraction," the leading shadow who is currently holding Everett over his shoulder says.

Point B, what and where the hell is Point B? Fuck, had I not been listening when they discussed this earlier? It didn't matter, though; we were already running again, and this time further into the forest as we clumped together in a tight unit. Jei was holding my hand and dragging me close behind him as we ran in silence.

We hadn't been running far when I started to hear the flow of a river coming from our left side. It progressively started getting louder and louder until the trees opened up. We were approaching a wide river. The water was flowing fast as I silently prayed, we didn't have to swim through it. The current was so strong I doubted I could swim across, even with being a competitive swimmer. I didn't have to think too hard on the matter because the lead Shadow led us to a large military style raft that was equipped with an engine that had been tied off to a tree on the riverbank.

"Get in, we don't have much time," he said as he lowered Everett's unconscious frame into the raft before jumping in himself. The second Shadow was next. He lowered Dean gently, followed by Colson, Jei, and Stefan. After placing Colson in the raft, Arno quickly rushed over to me, grabbing my hand and yanking me in the raft with him.

Everything was happening so fast, before I knew it the raft was racing down the river, the icy cold air biting at my skin. Looking back at where we just left the riverbank, I could have sworn I saw a figure standing there watching as we made our getaway. I blinked a few times, thinking my mind was playing tricks on me, but there they were—standing on the river bank, unmoving, as they watched us disappear down the river.

We weren't on the river long, the steady current working in our favor as we soon beached on the sandy riverbank. Everything was so fluid as the guys moved with ease, grabbing each one of my guys and quickly exiting the raft, continuing on foot. Jei grabbed my hand once again as Arno was carrying Colson.

"Just up ahead, the jet is beyond this tree line." Our leader informed us as we broke through the forest into the field we had landed in earlier this evening. My immediate thoughts were with Cain and Stone. Were they here, too, or were they still in our second vehicle? Arno's sense of mind reading capabilities truly shocked me, because he instantly said to me, "Cain and Stone have been notified of the change in plans and will meet us back at the castle." We all made our way to the jet, each one of us running up the stairs and breathing a sigh of relief as our lungs tried to catch up with the adrenaline of what just happened. Jei took up the pilot seat and quickly started up the engine and had us moving in record timing. Dean and Everett had been placed to the front of the jet, the two Shadows working on patching their wounds as best they could for now. I quickly made my way to Arno who lay Colson down, towards the back of the jet where more supplies were readily available.

Arno said nothing as he went to work cleaning as much dried blood from Colson's skin as he could and patching every wound he came across. Arno's main concern was the bullet wound that was still oozing blood and now pus from the large hole it created. Colson's skin was pale, too pale. I cupped Colson's face in my hands once again and tried to wake him as Arno kept working on trying to stop the bleeding.

"Colson, please, please, wake up. Don't leave me, please." My eyes started stinging as tears started filling my eyes. There was no response. His head was heavy as I cradled it in my hands.

"Will he make it?" I looked at Arno as a sob slipped through my lips.

Arno said nothing, his eyes meeting mine, and a feeling of dread swept over me. I watched Arno make fast work of bandages as he applied pressure on the wound. Bandage after bandage he pressed to the hole, but each one becoming saturated as quickly as it was placed. I lowered my head to Colson's as tears started streaming down my cheeks. Resting my forehead to his, I couldn't hold it in any longer and started sobbing against one of the men who showed me what love felt like.

"We were too late; I'm so sorry," I whispered, my voice cracking as I apologized over and over to my lifeless Colson. *How is this happening?*

"Why are you crying, baby girl?" His voice was so low I thought I was dreaming. My eyes snapped open as a set of golden eyes stared back up at me. "Please don't cry," Colson said as he reached for my face and brushed the tears from my cheek. I leaned into his hand, continuing to cry as I held his head to my lap.

"Look at me, Sloan," he said, and I opened my eyes to him. His face was so drained of life and so pale. He struggled to breathe as the pain from his abdomen made it difficult for him to get a proper breath.

"Careful, mate, you've lost a lot of blood. Try not to move," Arno said to Colson when Colson tried getting up. I stroked his hair back and brushed my thumb over his cheek, not fully believing he was awake.

"I want you to know, you're the best thing that ever happened to me." Colson started to cough, and I placed one hand on his chest to try and stop his body from jerking with every cough. "You're the light that I never thought I would find. You brought me out of the pits of hell and showed me what love is. You're in good hands. They'll take care of you and love you the way you deserve. They—" I quickly cut him off.

"Stop talking like that. You're going to be fine; we're going to be fine. Just hold on a little longer for me." A cold hand cupped my cheek.

"You're so beautiful. I'm so sorry we brought you into this world. You deserve so much more."

My chest felt as though someone was squeezing the life out of my heart, not allowing it to pump blood properly. I swallowed, trying to ease the tightness in my throat as I attempted to control my sobbing. This isn't happening. I couldn't lose him. He was one third of my heart, and without him it would never feel whole again.

His hold on my face started to loosen, and I held his hand to my cheek.

"I'll meet you in the pool, baby girl." Colson's eyes started to flutter shut as his hand fell limp in mine.

"No, Colson, stay with me! Stay with me!" I dropped his hand and grabbed his face. His eyes closed and his head fell to the side. I gently tapped the side of his face with my hand as I frantically tried to make him open his eyes. He couldn't die, not like this. This isn't how our story is meant to end; our life had only just started.

"Colson! Open your eyes, please, open your eyes!" I was screaming now, shaking his lifeless body violently, trying to wake him, but he was no longer responding. I looked up to Arno, silently pleading with him to help me.

"Save him, Arno! Please, help him!" I begged as tears began clouding my vision. My world was crumbling where I sat. I was falling further and further into a darkness I was all too familiar with. Falling. Falling. Falling. I had slipped into this world of agony, clawing at the walls trying to escape, but it was no use. My once beating heart was now cold and slowly being engulfed by the inky blackness of the hole of pain I'd just entered.

"He's gone." Arno's whispers penetrated my core as the realization of Colson actually being dead seeped into my bones. Black dots started to form across my vision, and just as I was about to fall, Arno caught me and lifted me from where I sat. His strong arms cocooned me to his large frame as my head collided with his chest. My body was trembling as I collapsed into Arno's embrace and screamed my pain as I burrowed my face further into his chest. I screamed again and again and again, his hand resting on the back of my head as he let me break down, piece by piece. I was screaming for so long, my voice started to rattle and I quickly lost my strength to continue. Falling silently against his chest, I sobbed quietly as Arno brushed his fingers through my long hair, and soon exhaustion took hold of me. A blanket of eerie blackness engulfed me as I slipped into the darkest cavity of this earth, into the depths of the abyss. Colson was gone. Colson was dead.

CHAPTER 30

SLOAN

I'm swimming. Beneath the water, I release tiny bubbles from my nose as I drag my arms through the water while it pushes back against my force. My body is weightless as the cool temperature of the water leaves my skin peppered with goosebumps. I can hold my breath for a long time, longer than most. I would be an amazing free diver if I'm being honest. The water is so clear I can see the tiles sparkle against the sun reflecting off the surface of the water. Blue-and-white tiles line the walls of the pool around me as I push my arms forward and drag them back over and over again until I reach the end of the pool. Breaking the surface, I open my eyes, and I'm met with the familiar sparkle of golden eyes peering down at me.

Colson's tanned vibrant skin shines in the sun as

he lets his legs dangle off the edge, kicking them back and forth in the water. He's smiling at me, his dimples creating indents in his cheeks that make the butter-flies in my stomach awaken. I swim up between his legs as he wraps them around me, hooking his ankles behind me. He leans toward me, cupping my face with his hands, our faces are nearly touching. Just as our lips are mere millimeters from touching, a loud crack pierces the air, causing my ears to ring.

His touch disappears from my cheeks as a pool of blood erupts from his abdomen. Once vibrant eyes turn glossy and light-years away as Colson's gaze no longer reaches me. His presence fades, as does his body. A smokey image of him floats through the air as he slowly starts to leave me, disappearing as a ghost, a distant memory, taken from me as quickly as he came.

I awaken with a sharp gasp, as my breathing becomes rapid. I'm borderline hyperventilating. I call out for Colson, praying deep down the last twelve hours has all been a horrible nightmare. The room is totally dark except for a small beam of light that is shining from the cracked door leading to the bath-room. Sitting up, I clutch the blankets that are draped over me. I rub my eyes as I quickly try to adjust to the darkness and soon come to realize I'm in Everett's room in the castle, alone.

What the hell. I jump from my bed and race to the door, swinging it open and running down the hallway as fast as I can. Colson's room is at the end of the hallway as I pray to whomever is listening that he's fast asleep inside—untouched, unharmed, alive. I practically burst open the door as I throw myself through the threshold.

"Colson!" My voice is so strangely raspy as if I've been cheering at a college football game. My throat is sore with overuse. Dread fills my stomach as I quickly scan the room and find it empty. My eyes begin to sting as panic sets in, and I soon race to Dean's room as well, only to find it vacant as well. *Where the fuck is everyone?* The threat of tears begins to sting the back of my eyes as I hear the faintest sound of someone talking. Making my way to the hallway, I reach the stairs and hear many different voices coming from the kitchen downstairs.

I don't know why but I decide to tiptoe my way down the long staircase and quietly make my way to the entranceway to the kitchen.

"She's the strongest woman I've ever met. She did everything I asked of her and then some. Honestly, if it weren't for her, both of your asses would still be in Ireland and most likely dead," Arno spoke. I peeked into the kitchen, seeing Arno talking but couldn't see the others he was with. "I truly am sorry about Colson, mate; we should have gotten there sooner."

"Colson?" My voice cracks as the night before comes flooding back to me like a fucking avalanche. Arno turns to look at me, but it's the sight of Everett and Dean that has my legs collapsing beneath me as I fall to the floor. It had all been real, so utterly real. Colson is gone.

Before colliding with the stone tiles beneath me, I'm caught by a familiar pair of strong arms, lifting me into an embrace that holds me together before I can fall apart once more.

Dean's arms swallowed my small frame and held me so tight, as if he knew if he didn't, I would crumble into a million pieces. By instinct, my arms circled around his waist and held on equally tight. It wasn't just me who lost Colson—Dean and Everett just lost their brother. My feet suddenly left the floor as Dean grabbed my thighs. I wrapped my legs around his body, and then he carried me to the countertop and sat me down, still holding on to me tight. He buried his face into the crook of my neck and inhaled a deep breath, shuddering just a bit. He was aching inside; there was no doubt about it.

We stayed that way a long moment, the room utterly quiet as we just embraced one another. I never wanted to let him go in fear of him disappearing again. To my protest his grip on me loosened, and he reluctantly stepped away from me. Dean's face was completely discolored from the bruising he'd received. The whole left side of his face was swollen from his temple to his strong jaw. I rested my hand on the opposite side of his face, and he closed his eyes to my touch.

"Fuck, baby girl, I missed you," he whispered as he placed his hand on top of mine, his head pressing into the warmth of my palm. I inhaled a deep breath, about to respond, but he stepped back and allowed Everett a chance to embrace me as well. He stood between my legs as well, wrapping his arms around my shoulders. I pressed my head against his chest as he lowered his to the top of my head.

We stayed this way, our breathing becoming in sync with each other. The rise and fall of our breathing was soothing, as if we were two in one. My other half, my safety net, a third of my heart. Silent tears were streaming down my cheek and I let them, not wanting to move from this embrace to brush them away.

"I'm so sorry, Everett," I whispered, my choked voice barely letting me get the words out. Suddenly, it felt as though Everett stopped breathing. Our rising chests were no longer in the same rhythm. Everett's hands then gripped my shoulders, pulling me from his chest. I couldn't look into his eyes. Averting my gaze, I felt his hand rest on my chin, and he slowly tilted my face until I could no longer look away from him. His expression was so pained, so destroyed, I hardly recognized him as the Everett I'd known before. His eyes were glazed over, exhaustion evident in the dark circles beneath his eyes.

"Don't you apologize for anything, Sloan. None of this was your fault; none of this was anyone's fault, but mine." His shoulders slumped forward, the guilt weighing heavy on his beaten and bruised body. I shook my head, disagreeing with his statement but couldn't find the words to express that none of this was his fault. The lump in my throat was thick and restrictive, as I choked on a sob. I've never been much of a crier. I never cared for anyone enough to cry when something happened to them, but with them, my chest ached.

The room was silent as grief, and despair blanketed the four of us. It was eerie how a room that was totally silent was speaking so many words, expressing so much pain and loss without a single sound being made. Just as the silence was starting to be too much, Arno's voice broke me out of the trance, we were all in.

"I'm going to get a move on and head to headquarters and start tying things up. Take as much time as you all need; we will sort the details of Colson out when you're already." At the sound of his name, my chest tightened as images of his lifeless body flashed in my memory. Still sitting on the counter, I heard the shuffle of footsteps, Arno shaking Dean and Everett's hands before making his way in front of me. I looked up at the man that was once my enemy, but after the last twenty-four hours had quickly become what I would call, a friend.

Arno's face was equally as pained as the rest of us. His deep brown eyes stared into my soul with silent apologies. What he did next truly shocked me to my core. Arno reached up to my face and brushed a long strand of hair behind my ear, then cupped my face.

"I'm sorry, little one. I lied to you. I wasn't able to bring everyone home alive. For that, I can't apologize enough." Arno then hugged me. He hugged me tight as his words flooded my brain. My head was resting on Arno's shoulder as I peered over at Dean and Everett, who were giving each other a look of confusion. But at this moment, I knew I could trust Arno. Not only did he show his loyalty, but he also showed something even more. Arno showed that he had the capability of caring for someone other than himself. I knew he was now a friend to me, and I to him. I hugged him back, thanking him for all he'd done and for allowing me to have pieces of my heart brought back to me.

After our embrace, he gave my shoulder a friendly punch before saying, "I'm proud of you. You're more than just a little one; you're a fucking badass." Arno let out a small chuckle before leaving the kitchen. We all waited for the familiar sound of the front door closing as it echoed through the castle walls. I let out a breath I hadn't realized I was holding and lowered my head to the kitchen floor. It was then that I allowed myself to fall apart, to grieve, to shatter into a million pieces at the loss of Colson.

The three of us ended up in Colson's room that night. The three of us lay on his bed and allowed ourselves to feel the pain of losing him. Everett and Dean lost their brother, and I lost a piece of my soul.

The three of us slowly shattered as we became tangled in each other's limbs, holding tight to one another and never wanting to let go. We had to come to grips with the idea that we were no longer a family of four. We were now three and would always feel as though a part of us was missing. Colson was missing.

CHAPTER 31

SLOAN

The next few days passed in a blur. We spent most of our time at The Shadows headquarters being questioned and debriefed about the whole situation. The guys were gone for large portions of the days, being questioned and analyzed by doctors, therapists, and higher-ups, in regards to their captivity. While the guys were busy during the day, I was left wasting time throughout the headquarters. Mostly I would pass the time at the gym that was present in the building. I would find myself walking miles and miles on the treadmill allowing myself to feel numb and block the pain.

I started reliving the raid and trying to put together all the pieces—trying to understand what and how this had all happened. The guys were given a contact that would allow them to meet my step siblings in hopes of bringing us together. However, it all went sideways when the meeting was actually an ambush. Why? Why did they take my guys? This was what confused me the most.

The first morning with Dean and Everett, they informed me of all the details of their capture. They informed me that once they'd been brought into the building, they were locked in. Soon gas quickly filtered into the room, ultimately causing them to fall unconscious. Once they woke, they found themselves suspended by their restraints from the ceiling.

Sitting on the couch, I clutched a throw pillow as Dean and Everett then explained how they were beaten and tortured daily because they wouldn't give up my location. This tore me up the most—the fact that my guys allowed themselves to endure the most horrific torture one could imagine and not once give up my whereabouts.

Walking on the treadmill now, I go over all the details one by one in my head. They were taken by Cara and Cormac, my step siblings. They were then tortured to the extreme in hopes of them giving up my location. Everett also informed me that there was another character in this whole messed up shit; however, this person was never seen. There was a trap door in the floor of the building where this mystery person would hide while Cara and Cormac played as their puppet, doing everything imaginable to get my guys to talk. From power tools to whips, to knives. It was something straight out of a horror movie.

Then there was the figure on the side of the river-bank as we were escaping. This mystery person that wants me dead. I still hadn't mentioned this person to the guys; I'm not sure why. Thinking about it now, I made a mental note to tell the guys today. They needed to know every detail if we were going to find out who was doing all this.

It's safe to say the twins want me dead so I don't inherit any aspect of the Wallace family business. To think I want anything to do with that shit was the twins' first mistake. I wanted nothing to do with Shem's business, all I was hoping for was to meet and build a relationship with my family, and that was my mistake. To think anyone in my bloodline are good people is laughable, and I should have known I was never destined for a happily ever after. If I wanted one of those, I would have to build it all on my own.

The Shadows' tech specialists still were unable to find out more of a motive behind this attack other than the power-hungry twins, but something still was not adding up. Everett and Dean felt the same way. Had Shem known about all this captivity bullshit? Did he know the twins wanted me dead, so they would inherit his empire? These were the questions that I wanted answered too.

Apart from my questions needing answers, there was something I wanted more. I wanted revenge. Since escaping the compound, there's been a feeling of utter hatred coursing through my veins. A feeling I'm not surprisingly familiar with, given the treatment I'd received growing up at the hands of my parents. This feeling has started to manifest into something far stronger than I thought possible. Red. I see red whenever I hear or say the name "Cara." She's who I think about when the inky black begins swirling inside me. I see her face, her smile, her insanely familiar face that looks too much like my father's.

I want revenge. I want to stand in front of her and give her the same treatment she gave to my guys. I want her to feel the pain of loss as I rip away someone important to her. I began planning and plotting all the ways I will torture her—from plucking her fingernails off to carving my name into her porcelain skin. I'm changing. Changing in a way that most would, after watching the person they love die in their hands. I will find her, and I will kill her, but first I'm going to kill Cormac. I'm going to kill him right in front of her eyes.

"What are you thinking about, killer?" A voice startles me, almost causing me to fall from the tread-mill. I look over my shoulder to see Arno stepping up to the treadmill beside mine.

"Shit, Arno, you almost made me fall," I say to him, catching my balance and continuing my steady pace.

"That's why you need to be more aware of your surroundings and not be so deep in your head that you forget the world around you." His words rang true. Whenever I'm thinking of all the ways I'm going to kill Cara, I'm lost in thought. I'm lost so deeply that I completely shut out the world and fall into the abyss of pain and torture that I'm going to cause her.

"Firstly, you need to keep your emotions in check. You looked like you were plotting a world takeover just now. Secondly, I need you to fill me in on what you're thinking because I want in." Arno looks over to me with a devilish grin that I can't help returning. I've never had siblings before, obviously, but there is something about the way Arno and I have connected in the last few days. A way that sparks a sibling relationship type feel. I genuinely liked his company, which was a far cry from where we were not even one month ago. I'm thankful for him. An unlikely friendship from a more unlikely situation. Like I said, this was a movie plot if I've ever seen one.

I sighed and paused for a moment, Arno starting up his treadmill and beginning a slow walk beside me. I looked over to him, his eyes meeting mine as I confessed, "I want revenge. I want to kill the twins." The room was silent, and I half expected Arno to say something along the lines of "revenge gets you nowhere," or "revenge won't bring Colson back." Instead, he replied, "Right, let's get you trained up then."

I was shocked—speechless, actually. His response was so nonchalant, so matter of fact that I couldn't believe he was keen to my idea.

"Did you hear me right? I want to kill the twins?"

I asked him, continuing to stare at the side of his face as he picked up the pace of his walking.

"I heard you, little one, and I'm honestly shocked it took you this long to say it out loud." Arno turned and met my gaze, his expression hard to read. "They took from you the only good thing in your life; they deserve to die. Anyone that plans on hurting or possibly killing you deserves a fate worse than death, if I'm being honest. Let's get you trained up. Become a Shadow and get your revenge. Blood doesn't always mean family, and family doesn't always mean blood. What you have with the guys is something I will never understand, but you love them and they love you. That's worth fighting for and seeking revenge for. So, if you say you want revenge, then I'll help you. I wasn't lying before when I said you're a Shadow now. You're too deep into this world not to be one. Now, we just need to get you trained up."

I didn't know when I hit the stop button on my treadmill, but Arno's words ignited something inside me that I can't explain. I was a Shadow? Was I really, or just in the eyes of Arno? As if he were reading my mind, like all these Shadow employees knew how to do, he said, "I've spoken with the higher-ups that deal with recruitment. I've expressed my thoughts about you becoming one of us and how I saw something in you that night. You have something inside you that needs to be released. You've been caged too long; you've spent too long in the dark and have lived a life that no one should've lived. Your trauma is your strength. With that I see you succeeding in this life-style and so do the higher-ups. So, the choice is yours, Sloan. Do you want to become one of us, get your revenge, and live a life all your own?"

Was I ready? Was I able to become one of them? Become an Everett, a Dean, an Arno, or a Colson? Was I prepared for this? I didn't give myself a moment to hesitate.

"Yes, I'm ready," I responded. The laugh that came from Arno was pure mischief as he stopped his tread-mill and jumped off his track. Clapping his hands together, he tilted his head to the door before saying,

"Well, let's get this party started then, shall we? The guys are going to love this!"

Wait, what guys? My guys?

"Wait, what do you mean the guys will love this?" I said, following close behind him, but he just ignored my question as we left the gym.

———

"No way, no fucking way, Sloan. Arno, what the fuck, man? Why put this in her head?" Everett was pissed. We met Everett and Dean in the large lounge room, which had three massive brown leather couches, a mini kitchen, snack machines, and a large television mounted on the back wall.

"It's a smart move, mate. This will allow her to properly defend and protect herself. Fuck, I mean, look how many times someone has tried to kill her already," Arno said, speaking directly to Everett as I cuddled into Dean's side, his arm draped over my shoulder.

"I have to say I agree, love. This isn't the life I would have chosen for myself," Dean whispered in my ear as Everett and Arno continued butting heads with the idea of me becoming a Shadow.

Our fingers intertwined together as I looked up to meet Dean's face. "I wouldn't have chosen the life I've been living if I had the choice. With this at least I can protect myself from all the demons who seem to hunt me."

Dean's eyes were understanding, but I could still see he was apprehensive about the whole idea. He placed a kiss on the top of my head and said nothing more.

"Listen, mate, she's been through more than most people go through in their lives. She's handled everything that's been thrown at her. She wants this, and I know she will succeed."

I smiled at Arno's confidence in me.

"When the hell did you two become best friends anyway?" And there it was, the question I knew Everett was dying to have answered. Arno looked at me, not responding right away.

"When he decided you were worth saving for my happiness," I said. I was right, Arno didn't have to do anything for me or, better yet, save the men who literally kicked the shit out of him a few months prior.

Everett pinched the bridge of his nose, soaking in

my words and trying to come to terms with everything.

"I appreciate your help, mate. I really do. I also appreciate your taking care of our girl when we couldn't. I'm grateful. I just don't see how involving her in Shadows' business is in the best interest." Everett was scared. I could feel his tension as he brushed his hair back with both his hands. His whole demeanor was off; he was fidgety and couldn't stop pacing the room. The usual calm and collected Everett was now confused and torn.

Standing up, I made my way over to Everett and placed my hands to his chest.

"Everett, I can do this. I've never been surer about anything in my life. I want this for me. I want to be able to protect myself and those around me to the best of my ability. I want to live a life worth living and not depend on you and Dean to always protect me. I appreciate you both, but let me do this and let me get my vengeance on the twins. For Colson."

His hands found both sides of my neck as his thumbs rubbed against my jaw. The turmoil swirling in his eyes was evident. He was uncomfortable with this idea, but understood why I wanted this.

"We do this together then, the three of us." Everett pressed his lips to mine and kissed me so fiercely I could feel his concern with the sheer force of his lips. I kissed him back, opening my mouth to his and welcoming his tongue with an equal ferocity. I could have stayed in that moment forever. Our lips collided, teeth clattering and tongues fighting, but I pulled back and looked at him, our foreheads pressing together.

"The four of us," I reiterated. Everett looked over my shoulder to Arno who, I assumed, was still on the couch. A small chuckle came from behind me, and I knew it was Arno stirring the pot.

"Knock it off, Arno. I can easily change my mind," I said, not looking behind me.

"Not a word, little one," Arno responded from behind me. A deep sigh came from Everett, again hesitant on this whole arrangement. He closed his eyes and tilted his head back.

"Fine, the four of us. But he's not moving in with us." I smiled at Everett, shaking my head, agreeing with him.

"Yeah, I don't think you have to worry about that one. I quite like my house better if you don't mind. Don't want to overstep the terms of our new friendship now, do I, mate?" I turned to see Arno standing from the couch and straightening his shirt. I shook my head in his direction, giving him a crooked smile before he turned on his heel and left the three of us alone. Who would have thought I would become good friends with Arno? Certainly not me, but the world has a funny way of playing out for us. I suppose Arno was meant to be my ally after all, that crazy fucking bastard.

CHAPTER 32

SLOAN

The day I'd been dreading finally arrived. It's the day of Colson's funeral, and I'm not emotionally ready for this goodbye. Everett, Dean, and I are quiet this morning. We've returned to our house closer to the Shadows headquarters since we've found ourselves at the Shadow's remote facility more and more lately. We've all been sleeping in Colson's room since returning, the three of us huddled together trying to imagine this all being a terrible dream and hoping Colson will walk through the door any minute. But he never shows up.

In my bathroom, I've reapplied my makeup four times before I call it quits and accept that these tears will continue to flow throughout today. I slip into my long black dress, a small slit exposing my lower left leg as I bend over to strap on my black heels.

Standing up, I adjust the soft fabric and pull the string strap that keeps it from falling off my shoulder. It's a gorgeous dress, simple, yet flattering. This is the type of dress I would imagine myself wearing on a date, a date with Colson maybe. A date I will never get to experience.

My eyes begin to fill with fresh tears when I see Dean from the corner of my eye enter my bathroom. He's in an all-black suit, a black long sleeve button up underneath his black jacket, and his gun holster peeking through his opened jacket. The bruises on his face are still noticeable, but instead of the deep bluish-back coloring, they've now changed to a slightly greenish tint. His hands are in his pockets as his eyes roam up my body and rest on my face.

We don't say a word, just meet each other in the middle, our bodies colliding in an embrace of deep sorrow. I can't imagine losing a brother I've known almost my whole life, but the pain of losing Colson after knowing him less than a year, is painful enough. The hole in their chests from losing a brother is black, deep, and forever scarred inside both their chests.

I can feel a tear land on my shoulder as Dean inhales a deep breath. He's trembling just slightly. I can tell he's holding in his true emotions, not wanting to fully break down.

"You've saved my life twice now, Sloan; you've fucking saved me." Dean's voice is hoarse as though he's been crying for a lot longer than just now. "I'm sorry for everything, and I agree with you." He pulls back from our embrace and continues. "You should become a Shadow. You're the strongest person I know and more than capable of protecting yourself." Dean's thumb brushes away a tear from my cheek.

I close my eyes, soaking in his words as he continues brushing my cheek with his thumb. "I love you, baby girl," Dean's lips touch mine, so tender, so soft I melt into his mouth as we kiss the pain flowing between us. Strong hands brush through my long blonde hair, holding my head to his as we step in closer to each other. His large frame slowly pushes me against the vanity as our mouths continue devouring one another.

Time starts to slow down, the once thunderstorm raging inside my chest only a moment ago is now a distant memory. Dean's touch grounds me; it brings me from the edge of destruction and shows me the peace in the moment. I'm no longer falling when I'm in his arms. This is the power Dean holds; he is the master (whether he knows it or not) at saving me from my inner turmoil. I wish this was how I felt every second of every day, but the moment his lips leave mine, I'm quickly brought back to reality. I'm brought back to the moment when we're both getting ready for a funeral. Colson's funeral. We stare at each other; a silent pep talk that we'll make it through this. We've already made it through more than most, and we'll make it through this too. As painful as it is, and will continue to be, we will do this together.

"Are you ready, love?" Everett's voice travels

through the bathroom, startling me as I turn to face him. He's dressed similarly to Dean, in an all-black suit. His face is utterly neutral, giving away no emotion that he, too, is hurting inside. Everett places his hands in his pockets as he looks between Dean and me.

"No words I say will ever bring Colson back, but I'm sorry to the both of you. I should have been more prepared. I should have never let my guard down. I wanted so badly to give you the family you deserve, and I went against everything I was trained to do. And now Colson is dead. Colson is fucking dead!" Everett punched the wall, his fist disappearing into the drywall as he screamed in frustration.

I flinched at the sudden eruption, putting my hand over my mouth while I watched Everett's knuckles drip with blood as he pulled it back through the wall. Dean tossed him a hand towel that was hanging beside the mirror and Everett caught it without even looking up. Wiping away the blood from his fingers, he says, "We better leave now if we want to make it there on time." Everett turned on his heels and left us standing in the bathroom once again. My chest heaving from the shock of what just happened.

"He'll be okay. This is how he deals with things. He blames himself for a while and then gets his revenge sooner or later. Come now, let's get moving." Dean placed his hand on my lower back, ushering me out of the bathroom. Making our way to the garage, I noticed Everett was already in the driver's seat, waiting for the two of us. His head was resting on his fist that was leaning against the window. Lifting his head, I caught a quick glimpse of him wiping away a lone tear. He was crying.

CHAPTER 33

SLOAN

Stepping out of the Range Rover, a warm breeze hits my face, tousling my hair over my shoulders. I close my eyes to the sudden feel of the fresh air and inhale deeply before I open my eyes to the awaiting cemetery in front of me. The Shadows have their own private cemetery behind their headquarters. The plot is beautiful. It's completely fenced in by a four-foot-tall black iron clad fence with sharp points at the top of each post. The grass is exquisitely green, each stone hedge identical to the next, lined up in perfect rows. They're small stones with a curved top. The only scripture being the person's name and their birthdate along with the date they passed. Nothing else, no memory of who they were, no labels if they were a husband, sibling, son, nothing, just a name and a date. It makes the whole thing so much less personal.

The three of us are walking through the small

gates, the sound of the wind the only noise invading my ears. I'm skimming through each stone, keeping my eyes busy and not wanting to look forward. I know it's coming, though; I can see it in my peripherals. A long black coffin lies in front of us. Colson lies in front of us. We reach the edge of his coffin, and I can no longer delay the inevitable. I look up, my eyes landing on the lone coffin perched on a stand, next to a large rectangular hole in the ground. My heart feels like it's stopped beating; it hurts.

As much as I don't want to admit it, he's gone, and I now can't stop looking at his final resting place. I begin to wonder, is he comfortable? Is he hot or cold inside the coffin? Is his soul still with him, or is it already gone to wherever our souls go when we're gone? Did it hurt?

We are the only ones in the cemetery—Everett, Dean and me—and the world feels as though it's stopped spinning. The three of us stand around his coffin, not saying a word. I fiddle with my hands in front of me, trying my hardest to remain strong, to allow the guys to mourn and not worry about me. They've both lost their family, their friend, their brother. I hold in my emotions so the guys don't feel the need to try and comfort me; I want this moment to be a closure for them.

I start taking long, slow breaths and focus all my attention on the steady inhale and exhale of my breathing. I look stoic on the outside, but inside there is a war raging deep in my core. I can't shake the feeling of guilt. This was my fault. They can deny it all they want, but deep down if it weren't for me trying to find my family, they wouldn't have gone to Ireland and this ultimately wouldn't have happened. Since they've met me, I have caused so much pain. From Dean's capture to now Colson's death, what's next?

I can feel the heat rising from my chest to my ears as my sorrow turns to rage. This won't go unpunished. I will have my revenge. I will get my revenge for Colson, for Dean, and for Everett. No one else is going to get hurt because of me. I will make sure of it.

I look up from my hands and see Everett placing his hand on top of Colson's coffin. His eyes are closed and his expression is painful. His dark eyebrows are pinched so tight, and his lips are pressed into a thin line, but I catch a small quiver from his bottom lip. Everett is a strong man; there's no denying that, but he's hurting and still he fights the battle with his emotions. They say men don't cry, but seeing a man cry, especially in a circumstance like this, only shows their true strength, but he never falters. Everett remains still, not allowing even the threat of a tear to escape his gorgeous green eyes. Inside I wish he would. I wish he would allow his tears to flow. Get out the sadness and allow his body to feel the loss, only then can he move on.

Dean approaches Everett, standing behind him, and rests his large hand on Everett's shoulder. He bows his head and closes his eyes.

"From the shadows to the light, until we reunite. Rest easy, brother." Dean's words break the dam holding back my tears, and they begin to stream down my face. Dean and Everett embrace one another in a hug that speaks volumes. They're both devastated and rightfully so. I then hear a sound of footsteps coming up behind me, and I turn to see Arno making his way over. Following him is Stefan, Jei, Caine, and Stone, all dressed in black as they approach the three of us.

No one speaks. They all take turns touching their hands to Colson's coffin and reciting the same phrase Dean said. From the shadows to the light, until we reunite. A short phrase that brings so much meaning to the lives they all live. They are considered Shadows —they walk, talk, and breathe darkness. Passing over to the unknown is a source of peace, their source of light. There's a special place reserved for these men in the afterlife. I'd like to hope they reach heaven, but with what they do, would God forgive them, even when the people they execute are bad? I imagine they have their own special place waiting for them, a place full of light, warmth, and endless peace. The Shadows in the light. The place worth striving for.

I close my eyes and say under my breath, "I love you, Colson. I love you now, I love you always, I love you forever."

I open my eyes and see Everett standing in front of me, looking down at my now tear-soaked face as he raises his hand to my chin.

"He loved you, Sloan. He loved you so fucking much." Everett wraps his arms around me, squeezing me tight, the both of us needing each other while we say our final goodbyes as the coffin is slowly lowered into the ground. Dean comes to my side as Everett and I part. Dean threads his fingers through mine, standing beside me, as Everett does the same on my other side. The three of us stand there, connected as one, watching as the coffin disappears from our view.

I squeeze both my guys' hands a little tighter as Arno and the rest of the guys begin shoveling the large mound of dirt atop the coffin. We stand there until the entire hole is covered and now only looks like a freshly disturbed piece of land. The wind stills, and a burst of cool air blows past us so hard it takes the breath from my lungs. It's quick and sudden, and I can't help thinking it was Colson saying goodbye to us, to his brothers, to this world.

"Goodbye, brother," Everett says.

"Goodbye, mate," Dean says.

Another cool burst of air hits us, and I can't help but smile knowing he's no longer in pain, no longer fighting his inner demons. Colson's at peace, and I know he's here with us, reassuring us that he's okay. He's free.

We all head inside the headquarters' building. My heart still aches with the fact I will never get to touch him again, never hold his hand, never go swimming with him, at least not in this life. We sit in the large lounge room, but there is little conversation. Mainly the guys talk about past training memories and missions they had with Colson. Everett and Dean are smiling, talking about all the shit the three of them used to get into while sipping on their whiskey and slowly feeling the effects of the alcohol. I sit on the couch and watch the interaction amongst the guys.

So many memories, so much laughter, and so much love Colson brought to this group of men. They met under terrible circumstances, but they built their own family amongst themselves. They experienced trauma and heartache unlike anyone else in this world, and yet they bonded over their pain. They created this brotherhood that I can only admire and envy. Even when they hate each other some days, they also care for one another. I smile again to myself, thinking about how Everett, Dean, and Colson literally kicked the shit out of Arno, Stefan, and Jei, yet here they are, laughing about memories they shared, all because of this fucked up world they live in.

"What's that smile for, little one?" Arno says to me, plopping down on the couch beside me. I turn to face him, my cheeks red and puffy from crying, and smile as I answer him.

"How my guys quite literally beat the shit out of you only a few months ago, yet you helped save them. Not only you, but Jei and Stefan as well."

Arno tilts his head to the side, turning and looking at Everett and Dean who are talking near the built-in fireplace across the room. "It's a man thing, I suppose. We beat the piss out of each other one day and save each other's ass the next. And when there's a girl involved, no telling what we'll do." Arno takes a swig from his whiskey and looks towards Everett and Dean. "It was Colson who started the tiff between my guys and your guys. Cheeky bastard, that one. One day at Stone Fortress when it was still the training center for recruits, Colson thought it would be funny if he poisoned one of the instructors' coffee one morning. He and that specific instructor butted heads daily, and Colson had had enough. Instead, he put the mixture in my coffee, and I spent the next four days puking and shitting my brains out in the hospital wing."

I couldn't help the laugh that escaped from me.

"That's what started the war between his team and my team. Every day after that we tried to one up each other from being the best at hand-to-hand combat to long range shooting. We competed in everything." Arno paused a moment looking into his crystal tumbler, swirling around the amber liquid before continuing. "If I knew that coffee was poisoned, knowing what I know now, I think I would still have drunk it. From that point on, we had something to look forward to in that place. Even if that meant plotting our next move against those three bastards."

We sat there together on the couch in silence for a while, both of us lost in our thoughts as the room started filtering out slowly until it was just Everett, Dean, Arno, and me left. Everett and Dean made their way over to our couch, Dean offering a hand to me and helping me stand. Everett did the same to Arno except in a more manly way, clapping hands hard and pulling Arno to his feet in one swift motion.

"I haven't properly thanked you for saving us. Not only for saving us, but taking care of our girl," Everett raised his glass to Arno, and they clinked together their glasses before tipping them back and finishing the remaining contents in one gulp.

"She gave me no choice; she threatened my life if I didn't help her get you bastards out. I'm just sorry I wasn't there in time." Arno's words were sincere as he looked over at me, his expression apologetic. "She's a strong one, I'll give her that. You've got your hands full with this one, mate." Arno clapped his hand on Everett's shoulder, and they both let out a snort of a laugh. Without saying anything else, Arno turned and started his way to the door.

"She starts her training Monday. We'll need you to teach her all the nerdy tech shit you do," Everett called out to Arno, making him stop in his tracks. I looked up to Dean at my side who was looking down to me with a crooked smile, nodding once in agreement. I was going to become a Shadow. "Already got it approved from higher-ups. She's our responsibility, and we say when she's ready, but since you suggested this plan, you're coming along for the ride."

Arno turns around, a devilish grin splayed across his face.

"Plus, she'll need a face to punch when she learns

hand to hand," Dean chimed in, wrapping his hand around my waist and squeezing my hip just enough to awaken the butterflies in my stomach. Arno placed his hands in his pants, sweeping his gaze over the three of us and nodding his head at the same time.

"Right, let's get you that revenge, little one." Arno winks at me and salutes the guys before exiting the lounge. A sense of power ignites in my chest. I can do this. I will earn my revenge, and I will learn from the best. Time to get to work.

CHAPTER 34

SLOAN

Making our way back to the house, we decide in the car that what we need is a good ole fashion movie night equipped with popcorn, soda, and pizza. Dean ordered the pizza while in the car, so it only took five minutes to arrive once we got to the house. We each made our way to our rooms to change out of our clothes and into the mandatory attire for the night, sweatpants for the guys minus their shirts and my usual silk shorts and matching tank top. We all rendezvoused in the living room, the pizza and soda already on the coffee table, while the popcorn began popping in the microwave.

Dean was already inhaling a slice of pizza, his legs spread wide on the couch and an open beer in his opposite hand. I almost made it to the couch, but the reflection of the moon against the pool had me stopping in my tracks. Images of Colson and me flashed across my vision, and my stomach tightened at the memory. I closed my eyes, trying to remain in the moment, but it was Dean's confession that had me laughing.

"He didn't even know how to swim," Dean's voice was muffled by a bite of pizza, but I immediately turned to face him.

"You're lying, of course he knew how to swim," I respond. A smile creeps across Dean's face.

"He's right, the bastard never learned to swim, and the little he did know was taught in training. He tried and tried but never could get his arms and legs to work together properly," Everett said, coming up behind me and wrapping his arms around my waist and burying his face in the crook of my neck. I placed my hands on Everett's forearms and laughed so hard that tears started to form in my eyes.

"I can't believe he couldn't swim. He fooled me," I said to both of them.

"He was too busy doing other things to you in the pool than trying to convince you he could swim." Dean looks over at me and gives me a wink and I just laugh. It felt so good to genuinely laugh. I couldn't remember the last time I had. Everett and I join Dean on the couch. I sit in the middle between my two guys, two pieces of my heart, my family.

We ended up watching a few episodes of *The Office*, all of us deciding we needed humor for the night, and it was truly perfect. We laughed at the ridiculous scenes between Jim and Dwight, and we each said, "That's what she said" at least once throughout the night. I ended up laying my head in Everett's lap, while my legs rested across Dean, who soon started massaging my calves while Everett brushed his long fingers through my hair, gently scratching my scalp. This was home.

I fell asleep at one point. Last I remember, I was watching Jim and the rest of the crew trick Michael by turning the clocks in the office forward so they could all go home early. Classic. I woke up in Colson's bed, Dean lowering my head gently to the pillow. The three of us found ourselves in this room every night since coming home. Neither of us wanted to sleep anywhere else but here.

Everett removed his sweatpants and climbed into the bed beside me in nothing but his boxers, while Dean did the same on the opposite side. I turn onto my stomach and wrap my arms around Colson's pillow, inhaling deeply. It still smells like him, cedar wood and clean linen. Two scents so opposite yet such a delicious combo. I inhale again, knowing the guys are watching me, yet I don't care in the slightest.

A strong hand snakes up my back, beneath my tank top, and starts gently drawing lines up and down my back. It tickles slightly, making the muscles in my back tense just a bit, but it feels so relaxing. A small moan slips from my lips as another hand starts massaging my ass. My skin is tingling beneath their touch, a wave of pleasure building in my stomach.

Another moan escapes me, and I'm met with a gentle slap to my ass.

"Keep making those noises, love, and I can assure you there will be no sleeping tonight," Everett's words are a threat, but I can't help myself when a third moan travels up my throat. That's all it took. Everett grabbed my shorts, ripping them in two in a swift motion.

"Hey, those were my favorite pajamas," I say, lifting my head from the pillow. I hear Dean laughing quietly at my back while Everett delivers another slap to my ass.

"I warned you. Besides, I've missed the fuck out of you." His voice is dripping with desire, and I turn towards Dean to see his eyes roaming my exposed side boob and licking his bottom lip with hunger.

"You keen, mate?" Everett asks Dean, and his response is a deep, throaty growl as he tears my top from my body as well. They're both wild with need as Everett grabs my legs, flipping me to my back so suddenly. I squeak in surprise. Dean's mouth is quickly over mine, inhaling my breath and kissing me with the force of a tsunami. His strong lips claim mine as if I'm his lifeline, and I'm the only thing holding him to this earth. I grab the back of his head, clutching his grown-out hair in my grasp and hold him even tighter to my face. I scratch his scalp hard, making him groan into my mouth.

Everett started kissing my abdomen, licking and nipping as he ventures lower. His tongue stops at the apex of my groin sucking and kissing the tender post just above my clit. I shudder from his warm breath against my skin and arch my pelvis to his face, my mouth still drowning in Dean's lips.

Dean's hands cup my breasts, pinching and rolling my nipples between his fingers. My body ignites from their touch, electricity surging through my body with every kiss, every touch they deliver. I'm floating in bliss when Everett's tongue dips between my folds, and I cry out. My screams are absorbed by Dean's mouth as he smiles against my mouth.

"She likes that, mate. Keep going, but don't let her come just yet." Dean's voice is all sex, all lust. His hand wraps around the front of my neck and squeezes gently as his tongue enters my mouth once again. I'm lost to them, completely and utterly lost to these two men devouring me. I'm their own personal buffet and they're starving.

Everett's tongue continues to swirl around my clit, making me see stars, but it's not until he introduces two fingers inside my soaking pussy that I'm thrown over the edge of pleasure. I writhe beneath him, unable to stop my body from squirming as he pumps his fingers in and out of me. Dean pulls his face away from mine, and I fall back to the pillow, drawing in the feeling of Everett's tongue as he brings me to the point of an orgasm that's been steadily building in my core. I can feel the bed dip beside me as Dean moves around, but I'm totally lost in the moment of Everett's tongue and am about to come.

My breathing picks up as small beads of sweat dip between my breasts.

"Oh God, don't stop, I'm right there," I say, my words breathy and trembling as I chase my orgasm. Just as I'm about to fall into the sea of euphoria, Everett pulls away. I'm suddenly completely empty, and the pain of my lost orgasm is too much.

"No, don't stop. Fuck, I'm almost there," I beg as I lift my head from the bed to look at him. I'm met with Everett smiling down at me as he pulls his boxers down, his erection springing out as he grabs himself and starts stroking up and down.

"You come when we say, baby girl," Dean whispers in my ear, giving me chills. "Now, open your mouth for me." I turn my head to face him, and I'm met with his cock, hard and ready for me as he gently pushes the head between my lips. His velvety smooth cock invades my mouth, and I start sucking, making him moan above me. He's so big, I can't take him all in, so I wrap my hand around his base and start pumping my hand in sync with my lips.

"Fuckkkk," Dean moans out as his hand threads through my hair and pushes me with every pump to take him deeper.

"Don't move, sweetheart. Stay still for me," I hear Everett, but I can't see him. My eyes started to water from Dean's cock going deeper and deeper down my throat. I let out a moan that allows my throat to open up even more.

"Holy fuck, do that again," Dean rumbles as his

cock twitches inside me, and I moan again, allowing his cock to hit the back of my throat. Dean's fist in my hair tightens when I suck him hard. I lock my lips around his thickness and suck like he's a fucking lollipop. Just then I feel Everett brush his cock against my entrance, teasing me with anticipation. Just the feeling of his tip has my orgasm building once more.

Just when I'm about to scream at him to fucking fill me up already, he fully seeds himself inside me with one hard forceful thrust, and the room starts spinning.

"Fuck, mate, a little warning next time. I don't want her biting my dick off," Dean's words sound so far away as I writhe in pleasure with my mouth utterly full with his pulsing cock.

"I said hold on, fuck what else do you need." Everett starts pumping inside me, intensifying the waves of my orgasm as he finds his rhythm. They both find a rhythm, together. Dean fucking my mouth while Everett fucks my pussy, and I'm slowly dying with pleasure. Dean pulls out for just a second to tell me he's about to come and asks if I'll swallow him. I don't even hesitate; I suck him back into my mouth, hoping that gave him his answer.

He pumps into me hard and deep; my gag reflex being pushed to the brink. Just when I'm about to come up for air, his warm seed shoots down the back of my throat. I swallow all the saltiness of his cum, causing another orgasm to rise when he growls out his release.

"Fuck, baby girl, you take me so well." Dean's words are hoarse and raspy as he slowly pulls out of my mouth, brushing his thumb across my bottom lip in satisfaction.

"Goddamn, that was hot," Everett says, pulling my attention back to him. His emerald eyes hypnotize me as he thrusts faster inside me, his orgasm building fast. He licks his bottom lip as he watches his cock go in and out, in and out, out bodies slapping together.

"Everett!" I yell, my second orgasm evident by the slickness between my legs. He slams his cock into me, and I drop my head back, moaning as I fall to pieces, my body convulsing with pleasure. He erupts inside me; his cock begins pulsing his release and strong hands squeezing my hips as if to hold himself steady. There will definitely be bruises from his hands tomorrow.

Everett stays inside me for a moment longer, his cock twitching a few more times as he comes down from his orgasm. A hand brushes my hair back from my face, while Dean's thumb tilts my chin to his face. His lips find mine as we kiss, so gently, so soft, and so passionately I don't even realize when Everett falls down beside me, wrapping his arm around my waist.

Dean kisses me a moment longer, then proceeds to lay down on my other side, the three of us panting, sweating, and dazed from our post euphoric orgasms. I feel the warmth of Everett's release drip between my legs, and I know I can't sleep until I shower. I sit up, looking between both my guys, a smile sneaking across my lips. I lean in and kiss them both before proceeding to head to Colson's bathroom and turn on the shower.

I stare at myself in the mirror, watching the condensation from the steam build from the top and working its way down. My hair is disheveled and knotted from Dean's hands. My hips are sore from Everett's grip, and I smile at the evidence of our wild escapades. I lower my head to the ground, shaking my head as I smile harder until something catches my eye underneath the counter.

I kneel down and see it's a hair tie. Not my hair tie, but Colson's. He always wore specific elastics in his hair; they were seafoam-green and made into a braided pattern. They were made to look like regular bracelets, but they're stretchy, allowing you to wear them as hair ties. I pick it up and spin it over and over in my hand, remembering how quickly and fluid he was able to put his hair in his typical man bun. There was something so sexy about the way he did it. I pull the elastic on to my wrist and trace my fingers along the braid, remembering all that was Colson.

Looking back to the mirror, I see Dean's and Everett's reflections staring back at me. They are close, so close. They step in so both their chests are touching me. My eyes swell with tears for him, for his memory, for his life that was ripped away from us. We stay this way, the three of us looking at our reflections until the condensation completely fills the mirror, fogging our reflections.

Then without any words, we all step into the shower together, silently soaking in each other's bodies, washing away the tears, and refreshing our minds before climbing back into Colson's bed. We lie there, intertwined in each other's limbs, all of us smelling of Colson's body wash, and we each drift off to sleep. That's where I see Colson's beautiful face. I see him in my dreams, the only place I will ever see him again until I leave this life.

EPILOGUE

CARA

"'Ow de foock ded they all get away? De plan was to wait oehntil she came lookin fahr de goehys and grab 'er when she entered de room!" I say to my men, each one looking stunned and embarrassed. They all fucked up, and now I have no leaverage on how to get Sloan back here so I can kill her myself. "You all 'ad one foockin jahb, one!" Without giving them the chance to explain, I pull my desert eagle from my waistband and fire off four shots, killing my men, one by one.

Breathing heavy as their bodies start pooling blood around their pathetic and lifeless bodies, I place my gun back in my waistband.

"Feel better, now?" he says to me, his sly English accent making my pussy throb. I turn to face him, and he's leaning back in his chair, looking smug as fuck as he gives me his signature devilish smile.

"Impeccable," I breathe out with a sigh.

"I love the way murder gets you all hot and bothered." His tone is all sex as he rises from his chair and steps over to me in two long strides. He towers over me, causing me to strain my neck to look up at his beautiful face. His hands capture my chin, brushing his thumb across my jaw and kisses me softly.

"We'll get them, love. No need to cause premature wrinkles on your gorgeous face. Enjoy the chase, I always do," His lips meet mine, and I absorb his words. Enjoy the chase. I do enjoy the chase; however, I'm on a time limit here.

"I 'ave to fend 'er before Shem does, no point in draggin dis ooeht lahnger dan it 'as to."

"Who doesn't like a cat and mouse game?" he groans into my mouth, our teeth touching as he smiles. "My little devil, I love it when you talk dirty." We are suddenly interrupted by my brother, Cormac. He bursts through the door, looking all sorts of irritated when he sees us kissing. Cormac lets out a long sigh before saying, "You finished? We got some work to do." Cormac's voice makes my eyes roll as annoyance floods my core. Like I didn't already know we have work to do. My fucking twin couldn't be anymore thickheaded when it comes to the obvious.

"What de foock, Cara? Ded you kell all o' dem?" His eyes drift from each of the dead bodies scattered on the floor, his tone even more irritated when he looks up at me, seeing my half smile across my face.

"For foock's sake." He kicks one of the guards,

trying to rid himself of the anger now coursing through his blood. Cormac pinches the bridge of his nose, taking a few deep breaths before looking back towards us.

"De blahnde one died, but I dooehbt you care. Johestet know dey'll retaliate fahr dat. Dey aren't a pack o' regular goehys, Cara, dey are deir own mercenary cahrporation. Dey 'ave ahthers."

I interrupted him before he could continue his rant, "Den let dem send deir best goehys, we need 'er, we need 'er dead if we want dis family fahrtune fahr our own. Plus, we 'ave an insider, dat cooehnts fahr sahmethin." I turn to face the man I've fallen in love with this past year. A man who was once just a guard for the business is now the lock and key holder to my heart. I brush his hair back on top, giving him another kiss before turning back to my brother.

"Right, den let's 'ear it, what's de plan, mate? 'Ow do we get de girl wethooeht bein kelled in de prahcess?" Cormac crosses his arms as he speaks directly to the man now holding my waist with his hand. He pulls me in close before giving Cormac a death stare and responds, "We kill her resources; without her resources she is just another mouse in the trap." He gives me a small squeeze on my hip, his hand heating my skin with only a touch.

Cormac nods his head once, squinting his eyes at the both of us.

"Ow can I troehst you?" Cormac says, placing his

hand in his pants pockets and tilting his head up slightly.

I look up to my man, his eyes dark as his lips curl into a wicked smile. "Because, mate, I know my brother. See here's the thing with being twins, as I'm sure you're aware, we sort of share the same mind, the same thought process. If that makes sense. I can anticipate his every move. I know his weakness, and I can hit him where it really hurts." Callum pauses a moment, pulling me into his chest. "So be patient and enjoy the game while it lasts. Sloan will be dead in due time, but for you, I think your time is up."

Callum pulls his gun from his holster, firing off two shots into Cormac's chest, and I flinch at the sound of my brother's body hitting the ground with a loud thump.

"Then there were two," Callum whispers into my ear. The two of us, slowly taking over our empire, one dead body at a time. Sloan's days are truly numbered, you can count on that.

ACKNOWLEDGMENTS

To my readers, what can I say you are all truly amazing! The love and support I've received from book one, The Shadows, was more than I could have ever expected. You kept my spark and passion alive to continue on with this series. Thank you is not a strong enough word for the appreciation I have for all of you.

My incredible editor, Rosanna, you are a rockstar and this book wouldn't be where it is today without you. Thank you for coming along with me on this journey again.

Abigail, my amazing designer, I am so in love with your work. You never stop amazing me. Your ability to bring my visions to life is perfection.

Again, to every single reader who purchased my book thank you. I have been able to meet so many amazing new people in this book community who share their love for reading and I could not be more grateful for these new relationships.

On to the last and final book of The Darkness Trilogy! Wow I can't believe I'm writing book three. I have fallen in love with these characters, I don't know if I'm ready to part with them just yet. What do you think will happen next?

ABOUT THE AUTHOR

Rebecca is a newly published author who lives in North Carolina with her husband, two kids, and four-legged friend. You will usually find her escaping into her writing where her deepest and darkest thoughts are created for others to enjoy. When she is not writing she is either exercising, listening to audiobooks, playing with her kids, watching true crime documentaries or zoning out while thinking of all the ways to torture her characters. As most of us authors nowadays say, check trigger warnings before diving in. Thank you for being here!

Learn more about Rebecca Hamby at rebeccahambyauthor.com. Join her newsletter to receive updates, teasers, giveaways, and special deals!

www.ingramcontent.com/pod-product-compliance
Lightning Source LLC
Chambersburg PA
CBHW050315160726
48002CB00001B/45